HOLDUP

HOLDUP

TERRI FIELDS

SQUARE
FISH

ROARING BROOK
PRESS

NEW YORK CITY

SQUARE
FISH

An Imprint of Macmillan

Library of Congress Cataloging-in-Publication Data
Fields, Terri, 1948-
Holdup / Terri Fields.
p. cm.
"A Deborah Brodie Book."
Summary: Diverse teens each react differently to a busy shift at a Phoenix, Arizona, Burger Heaven on a busy Saturday night that culminates in a showdown with two armed robbers.
ISBN: 978-0-312-56130-7
[1. Hostages—Fiction. 2. Conduct of life—Fiction. 3. Robbers and outlaws—Fiction. 4. Restaurants—Fiction.] I. Title.
PZ7.F47918Hol 2007
[Fic]—dc22
2006017566

Originally published in the United States by Roaring Brook Press
Square Fish logo designed by Filomena Tuosto
Book design by Angela Carlino
First Square Fish Edition: 2009
1 2 3 4 5 6 7 8 9 10
www.squarefishbooks.com

ACKNOWLEDGMENTS

A big thanks to
- the sophomores of 2003: Lauren, Kate, Luigi, Michelle, and Olivia, who stayed late to read a first draft aloud and give feedback,
- teens who shared experiences of working in fast-food restaurants,
- Jeff for his help with Jackson/Alex,
- Lori and Rick for lots of encouragement,
- Mom for the book's final punch, and
- Deborah for being a great editor and Rosemary for helping me to find her.

To My Family,
always the center of my world

BREAKING LOCAL NEWS • BREAKING LOCAL NEWS

"This is Jillian Kwan, with a late-breaking bulletin from KNKV, Channel 16, with Valley news you can count on. Police are clearing an area in the vicinity of Cactus and Tatum, where they suspect a robbery gone bad may have turned into a hostage situation. Yet unknown is the number of robbers or hostages. The police are using bullhorns, trying to make contact with the robber or robbers.

"We'll update you as soon as further information becomes available. Meanwhile, stay tuned to Channel 16 for Valley news you can count on."

WORK

SATURDAY SHIFTS AT
BURGER HEAVEN

JORDAN

Finally—a day of freedom. No school, no work, no one pulling me in seven different directions at the same time. I allow myself the amazing luxury of sinking even deeper into my sheets. I'd forgotten how great it can be to do absolutely nothing.

It's still October, but my stress level is already soaring. I thought junior year was supposed to be the killer. Wrong. Senior year is going to be a hundred times worse.

I tried to keep it from happening, I really did, but when I said I didn't think I could manage so many Advanced Placement classes, my counselor shook her head. "Jordan, don't you realize the difficulty of getting into a selective college?"

"Yes, but—," I said.

"No *but* . . .," my counselor interrupted. "You want the rewards, you've got to work."

"But, I think—"

Again, my counselor: "Jordan, this high school doesn't have very many students who could realistically consider Stanford, but you can. Imagine that! Stanford! I am not going to let you throw away such a wonderful opportunity because of some kind of early senioritis. Someday you'll thank me for this."

So now my supersized class load devours me every day. And every AP teacher warns, "Don't even think of complaining about the homework. You signed up for this class! You had to know that you were going to have a couple of hours a night."

Trying to find a little breathing room, I told my parents that given my homework load, I didn't think I could manage an after-school job. My father frowned, reminding me, "You're not a child any longer. Do you realize how much the kinds of colleges you're looking at will cost? "

"Yes, but—," I said.

My father interrupted. "I've taken every overtime shift I could get so we could afford to put you through a top-notch college. But honestly, Jordan, don't you think you have some obligation too?"

"But, I . . ."

My father put his arm around me. "I know my daughter. She would never believe she shouldn't be contributing at least some part. Such a smart girl with such a bright future."

So Burger Heaven now counts me as part of their "friendly team."

And then there's basketball. When I said I didn't think I could play varsity this year with all my other commitments, my coach came unglued. "Do you realize how much this team is counting on your shot?"

"Yes, but I—"

And Coach cut me off. "That's exactly the problem. There is no *I* in *team*, right? How many times have you heard me say that! It's the philosophy that guides our team. We'll just forget you even came in to see me today, because we both know that you are not going to let your teammates down."

So I'm in the gym three afternoons a week for preseason training.

But somehow today, the cosmos has aligned itself in my favor. Dad's out of town, Mom's at a conference, there's no school, practice got canceled, and I've X'd myself out as available for work.

I don't know when or if another opportunity like this will come along, but I won't let myself think about that. Instead, I'm going to sink even deeper into these sheets and give myself the amazing gift of this one day to do absolutely nothing.

SARA

So, yesterday this really hot guy comes in with, like, the world's greatest smile aimed at me. And I mean, here I am, wearing this puke-green Burger Heaven uniform, and I'm thinking could I at least ditch the dweeby orange beanie before we're face-to-face? I mean, like, did they get the most color-blind loser to design these uniforms?

So, before I can get the beanie off, this guy, he's, like, standing right in front of me with these amazingly awesome blue eyes, and I sorta freeze until some robot voice in me blurts, "Hi, welcome to Burger Heaven."

"Why thanks, Sara," he says.

"You . . . you know my name?" I gulp.

He winks one of those so-sexy baby blues. "Well, I had a little help," and he points to my name tag.

I feel like some minus IQ. I can feel my face getting red, which, I am so sure, clashes with the orange beanie! I try to recover by flashing a smile and saying, "So . . . how can I help you—with—with—food?"

He gives me that megawatt grin again, and honest, the guy has, like, gorgeous teeth, and I'm, like, trying not to stare at that perfect face when he says, "My sister's named Sara too, only her name has an *H* at the end."

And that's when I so know that, even with the beanie, this stud puppy is interested in me. I've got to keep this conversation going until he asks for my number. At least there's no line behind him, so we can, like, just keep talking until it happens.

"Uhh," I say, "uhh, you know why I don't have an *H* in my name?"

"No, but tell me," he says.

I smile. "'Cuz, when my mom found out she was pregnant with me, she says it just knocked the *H* right out of her."

My stud man's eyes move behind me. I don't even have to turn around to know that Manager Phil must be there. Like, why do I have the worst luck in the world? I mean, no girl in her right mind would even consider a date with Phil, so, like, how would he ever consider cutting me a little slack here? And, like, he can even read my mind. Phil snarls, "I'll finish this order, Sara."

But I don't just give up. I mean, this guy is hot, and hot guys are not all that common at Burger Heaven. "Oh, that's okay," I say brightly. "You know how I always like to help our customers."

9

Phil just glares. "You go fill the napkin containers."

He, like, gives me no choice, and I feel like tripping him when he tells the guy, "Sorry about Sara. I'll have your order right out." And I am even more burned when Mr. Awesome Blue Eyes does not say one single thing about how he was the one who started the flirting, which is exactly what he did. No, he just walks out with his burger and fries, without even a backward glance at me. I jam all the napkins in one container. They're in there so tight that no one will ever get them out! It will serve people right for coming to this stupid place!

Then my loser boss calls me into the office. And I have to have another one of the manager/bad-employee talks. It's not like I haven't done this a few gazillion times before with other managers. Phil says he's blah, blah, blah, disappointed in me, and blah, blah, blah, and, like, what do I have to say for myself?

I point at a sign on the wall, noticing that my Passion Pink polish is chipped. I decide I'm so not buying that brand again. I tell Phil, "Right there, doesn't that sign say 'Friendly service by friendly folks'?" Then I sigh and shrug my shoulders. "I, like, don't get it. I mean, wasn't I just following the Burger Heaven motto and being friendly?"

Phil rolls his eyes. So I just roll mine right back at him and say, "Hey, last week I got written up for being impatient with customers. I mean, I'm sorry, but, like, what exactly do you want from me?"

I don't know why I even bother to ask. It doesn't

matter. I get written up again. I have to sign this little form that says the manager talked to me about an inappropriate attitude. What a joke! The whole thing means . . . just about . . . a big nothing. We all know that, but we play *oh, let's pretend it matters*. The loser managers who are going nowhere in life like to feel important. So we have these talks; they write me up, and I use the signed forms to blot my lip gloss, which, like, I don't even know why I bother wearing. I mean, they don't make a lip gloss color that goes with puke-green uniforms.

I mean, let me just say that I hate this place: the gross smell of the grease in my hair that manages to hang around even after I've shampooed twice with Spring Rain, and the so-uncool fit of the baggy uniform that makes me look like a size fourteen.

Oh, I know they don't want me to work here. And, yeah, I so want to get fired.

ALEX

I *am* a player—wimpy managers—watching this chick magnet in action—they're jealous. I don't blame them, but it means they're always busting my chops about rules. Rules are all they have.

Too bad that at Burger Heaven, the counter girls don't turn me on. Except Theresa. Sara's a joke. Jordan's Jordan. But Theresa—she had to know we were the only 10s in a store of employee 4s. And she wanted me. I know it. She stood at the first register—made sure her butt got framed just right for me to take it all in.

I picked right up on her come-on—but I took my time. Let her want me that much more. For a few days, I just watched that butt wiggle its hello. Then I headed out of the kitchen. I stood kind of close to Theresa, but not *creeped-out* close. "You must be wearing space pants today." She looked up at me, confused. I smiled, ready for the payoff. "Because your butt is out of this world."

But Theresa didn't play it back. Instead, she started giving me the silent treatment. Like I'm supposed to beg or something? I don't do that.

Then all of a sudden, we get slammed. Haven't got the grill fired up yet, so, I throw some water on to speed the heat. Maybe ought to try that on Theresa. Start grilling a bunch of burgers, when the grill shoots flames five feet high. Boss is gonna freak if he sees this, so I tank the fire with a towel. Burgers look kind of burned, but people won't be happy if they have to wait. . . . Add extra cheese, more relish . . . flip the frigging mess on buns and put it up on the pick-up counter. Hey—just another day of cooking at the Heaven.

Take a break for some smokes outside. Just as soon as I've got some bucks I'm out of here—going to Hollywood, baby! Why not? Johnny Depp had just as crappy a kid life as me, moved even more times, and he's doing pretty good now, even if he is kind of old.

I drop a couple burgers on the ground and call for my cat. Named him Socks because he's got four white feet but the rest of him's black. Lives in back of the Dumpster. Never had a pet before, but Socks and me—we're a lot the same. Living in garbage, but we're still survivors. And we look good—both of us make all the ladies want to cuddle.

It's Paulie's day off, but he comes round the corner, sees me—stops to talk. Tells me how Sara said she heard Theresa talking to the manager. Theresa doesn't want to work the front—wants to be part of the kitchen crew.

Doesn't make sense to me. No girls ever want to work the back grill. Too greasy. So it's not the grill Theresa wants . . . it's me. Well, fine . . . she played hard to get. Now she can wait till I say.

On Theresa's next shift—she's working the back, right next to me. I look her over real good. She wears stuff that smells great—makes me think, *the things we could be doing in the storage room during breaks*. But girl's got to be punished for jacking me around—she'll have to wait.

Two days, side by side slinging burgers—and still silence. It's enough. I'm done waiting. I reach over to that beautiful butt and grab a nice little pinch. I'm thinking she's thinking it feels pretty good.

And then *wham!* A whole steel ketchup container slams into my head. Man, I can't see much, but what I'm seeing is all red. And I'm hoping it's just ketchup, but my head hurts something awful. And I'm wondering if maybe it's blood.

So after my head gets bandaged, and the ketchup gets cleaned, the overall manager shows up. Not just the shift guy, but some big shirt. He yells at me about "sexual harassment." Says I better be on my knees she doesn't sue Burger Heaven, because if she sues, they don't have my back.

"What about her wearing those tight pants?" I say.

"No excuse!" The vein in corporate's neck bulges. "Rules. Rules. Rules!" He pounds the table. Warns, "If you ever break another rule, you are out of Burger Heaven forever."

Ooh, out of frigging Burger Heaven. It's not that this place is anything great, but I got bills to pay before I move to California. And I'm going to need some extra cash there because it may take me a few months to land a movie deal.

This job is easy money. So why get fired? I lay low and follow all their stupid rules.

Then this P.M. they call asking about me taking a shift tonight. Yeah, I need the money, but I already worked my maximum, and it's against the rules to get overtime. It bites, but I tell them the truth.

They don't even listen—they're too busy griping about being shorthanded in the kitchen for tonight. And so—just like that—*bam!*—they change the rules. They tell me to come on in. I'm here *off the books* tonight. Anyone asks, I never worked today. They'll pay me in cash at the end of the shift—nobody needs to know about my overtime. Hey, cash is good with me.

So I start my "not really here" shift, and *man, I can't believe it* when I see for the first time since the ketchup, me and Theresa are going to be in the back together. She starts swinging her little butt. And there's no ketchup next to her.

THERESA

Sometimes I have to smile at the stupidity of it all when I think of myself as a Burger Heaven employee. I mean, I'm a vegetarian who's entirely hung up on health. I believe you have to take care of yourself. If you don't, nobody else is going to do it for you. But here I am routinely handing out fat on a bun with a pathetic pickle and a wilted piece of lettuce as the meal's only vegetables. I tell myself, it's people's choice, and for whatever reason, they want to eat this lard. They're going to do it whether I'm here or not. I need a job, and this place always fits my hours around school or gives me time off when I have to have it for big school projects.

I work the front counter and hustle to get the orders out quickly. Even when a lady with biggie thighs asks me for two giant-sized orders of fries, I smile and hand her the lard-coated sticks. Even when a dad brings his kid in for dinner four nights in a row, I never mention a word about nutritional needs, and when the old guy already missing three teeth orders an extra-large soda, I don't open my mouth about sugar's effect on teeth and the way this man should protect the ones he has left.

I even suck it up and shut up when a girl my age complains to the manager that I gave her the wrong order, when she knows perfectly well that the order she got is exactly what she asked for. She's already eaten almost all of it before she "remembers" that it's wrong. I think me and her and the manager all understand that she's just after free food. But I hand her a new order anyway and watch her walk out the door with it because our Burger Heaven motto is "Keep the customer happy." And I do buy into that motto, but only to a point. I mean, I shouldn't have to take the harassment crap that gets dished my way.

When a customer comes to the counter, I always deliver the corporate greeting, "Welcome to Burger Heaven, what may I serve you today?"

But I hate it when some jerk answers, "How about your body in my bed?"

"The menu of Burger Heaven's food is on the wall" is all I ever say. Then I fold my arms and stare him down until he orders his burger, shuts up, and slinks away. But believe me, getting hit on gets old real fast, and unfortunately, I get hit on all too often.

Okay, so I do have a great body. I'm proud of it. I

exercise, I eat right, and I'm lucky. But I'm only here to hawk burgers and fries. Unlike Sara, who's always trying to figure out some way to make her uniform tighter or shorter or show more cleavage, I do nothing to enhance the sexless bagginess of mine. But it doesn't seem to matter—some jerky customers still can't get the message that my body belongs to me!

Finally, I ask to work in the back doing kitchen prep because I decide that, despite the fact that I would never actually eat red meat, the hamburgers themselves never harass. But my manager just hems and haws at my request. "You wouldn't want to get all greasy back there," he motions.

"I'd be okay with it," I say. "I'd really like the change." My manager shakes his head. He says he hopes I'll understand that they like to save the cooking for people who don't speak English so well. "Besides," he says, "you give the healthy glow that we like to have greeting our Burger Heaven customers."

I think he thinks that's a compliment, so I don't tell him that the only reason I probably have that healthy glow is that I never eat Burger Heaven food. Instead, I say, "Thanks, but I've been here for a while now." He and I both know that's an accomplishment, since some employees don't even last a week. I continue, "I know you want to keep your employees working here and happy." I take a deep breath. "And I hope my seniority means that I can move to the back."

The manager smiles, tells me they definitely do want

happy employees. He's so glad I let him know my feelings, and he'll see what he can do for me.

I leave our little meeting feeling good—glad I finally said something. But the next week, when I walk in, I see another new guy is working in the back. And my schedule shows me still at the first register all week. So much for having a manager who cares.

I'm still seething when two guys arrive at my register. One of them says, "Oh, yeah, she's a ten."

The other says, "Not so fast. We need to see all sides. Wait until she turns around so we can see her butt too." And they just keep at it; they're talking about me like I'm not even human.

Then suddenly, I swear it isn't planned, I see my hand throwing a forty-four-ounce, ice-filled Pepsi all over the worst one, and I hear my voice shouting, "Maybe this'll help you cool down a little!"

My manager is staring at me in open-mouthed amazement. I am a little amazed myself. My hand lets the now-empty cup drop to the counter. I feel very certain that the company doesn't like the employees assaulting the customers.

Mutely, I watch the scene continue to unfold. First, the still-dry guy starts making fun of his friend. Then the Pepsi-soaked one charges at his buddy. They run out of the restaurant half-wrestling, half-chasing each other. We all stand in silence for a minute. The boys don't come back, and the restaurant noise returns to normal.

The manager calls me to the back. He says he hardly

knows what to say to me. I try to explain why I did it, but I'm not holding out much hope that I won't be fired. They do send me home for the rest of the day, but amazingly, they still want me back the next afternoon after school. And when I get in, the manager tells me I'll be pleased to know that there has been an opening in the back.

So I stand here, tossing premade patties on the grill, hearing their sizzle. It's easy work, and I can keep my mind tucked away elsewhere. During busy times, sometimes, there's another griller back here, but we rarely talk. If it gets real slow, I can even get in some deep knee bends and stretches. Then I start getting shifts with Alex and his trashy mouth. I silently laugh at him because he's denser than dumb if he thinks I'd ever even consider going out with him. But one day, he just pushes it too far. His pickup lines have gone beyond gross. He decides to let his hands do a little talking for him, and I realize he's never going to shut up without some help. My fingers reach out for the steel ketchup container and deliver a message even Alex can understand.

When management gets it all sorted out, I get an apology about the harassment.

I also get a lecture about how I simply cannot throw food or drinks or condiments or objects if I want to work at Burger Heaven. That does make sense, so I apologize, and I promise I'll stop.

And they promise that Alex and I won't be working the same shift again. And we don't—until tonight.

MANUEL

The lady in the blue Mercedes pulls up to the drive-through twice a week or more.

Every time, she says into the speaker, "Hmmm . . . now what do I want?" And then she always orders one small fries with no salt, one medium Coke with no ice, and a regular burger with no sauce. And then she always adds, "Could you make it quick? I'm in a hurry."

"Sure thing," I say. Truth is that I'm way ahead of her. See, I know it's her by the sound of her diesel engine, and before she says even one word, I've got her whole order punched into the register and called into the grill.

By the time she's saying, "Could you make it quick?" the guys in the back are already handing out the order.

Burger Heaven's goal is one hundred and twenty seconds on the clock from the first punch on the register to the time the order is in the customer's hands. Only two minutes total, but I usually beat it. Nobody on the window is faster than me. If I can't pick out a regular by the sound of the engine, I've got the order going from the first glimpse of the car.

Okay, I know. I sound like some geek who gets off on playing games at Burger Heaven, but hey, I'm here a lot of my life, why not try to make it interesting? And I'm glad to get the money. I don't care that the guys think this job is lame. Yeah, sure, I'd rather be hanging out playing B-ball, but even though we joke about it, none of us is ever going to have the easy life of an NBA star or get any of the "toys" those guys get. We don't even have wheels to go anywhere. So let the guys laugh at me. Wait till they see me buy Eduardo's F-150 while they're still walking. Then we'll see who's laughing.

Besides, I really like some of the regulars at BH. I mean, when I'm sick of work, in comes Keith. He actually thinks Burger Heaven is the best place in the world, which makes me stop and improve my attitude. Then, of course, there's Mrs. Wilkins. She never treats me like some sort of an automatic order taker. In fact, she not only knows I'm a senior, but she keeps encouraging me to apply for college every time she's here. Once or twice, she even brought me some scholarship information. I've tried to tell her that I'm not going to college, but she only says, "You never know. Think about it."

So Burger Heaven isn't so bad. The uniforms are pretty cheesy, but wearing them means that my regular clothes don't have that Burger Heaven smell. I figure it this way. What's the point of complaining about the job? Hey, I'm here either way, and my truck account is growing with every day that I work. Might as well make the best of it.

JORDAN

When my cell started ringing, I ignored it and snuggled even deeper into my comforter. I was pretty sure it was Stephanie, but I was not going to give up this one day that was all mine. Stephanie had stopped me right outside English yesterday to inform me that I was the lucky replacement for our school's Mock Trial team because Matthew had gotten kicked off at the last minute. I told her I was not the right person—I didn't even know much about Mock Trial. She said they could fill me in.

Still, I tried to get out of it. I told her I really didn't have time because of work and basketball, but Stephanie didn't listen. She said, "It's only this week that will be intense. Competition is next Saturday, and it won't take any of your time after that."

I tried to explain that I really didn't think I was interested in becoming a lawyer, so Mock Trial really wasn't for me, but Stephanie only laughed. "Believe me, one Mock Trial does not make you a lawyer. Listen, Mr. Koerber says you're smart and reliable and to tell you that Mock Trial would look great on your college applications. Please. The team worked so hard on this, and now stupid Matthew has to ruin it. Please, please help us out?"

I didn't say yes. In fact, I made Stephanie promise to try to find someone else, but I had the feeling that she wasn't going to look too hard when she said, "I'll call you tomorrow when we need you for practice."

"Not when . . . if!" I yelled to Stephanie's back as she hurried to her next class. And sure enough, right on cue, the phone was ringing. Maybe if I just didn't answer, she'd at least look for someone else.

But then my cell phone stopped, and the house phone started ringing insistently. I glanced over at the caller ID on my bedroom extension, and then I remembered that it had broken a couple of months ago. I'd had no time to get it fixed or get another phone. I listened to the ring. Finally, the phone stopped, and just as I was about to appreciate the silence, it started ringing again. I stared at the phone. What if it wasn't Stephanie? What if something had happened to one of my parents? I reached over and picked up the receiver.

"Thank god. You're answering. You're the only employee who is." It was Maria. Even though she was by far my favorite Burger Heaven manager, I groaned, knowing what was coming next. "I know you wanted to be off today. That's why I called everyone else first. It's a madhouse here. We're short three workers. Please . . . "

So what could I say? I got up, got my uniform on, and here I am on the one day I promised to myself. When am I ever going to learn to say *no* and stick to it? Now, there's a question with absolutely no answer.

I pull into the parking lot, feeling as prickly as the cactus garden out front, and as I take my place behind the Burger Heaven counter at register three, I'm so mad at myself that I feel like crying. How could I have ruined my perfect day! But then Maria tells me how grateful she is, and I see the line of customers stretching almost out the door. Even Sara says that my being here should help keep the "animals out there" from storming the counter. So I try to tell myself that it wasn't such a bad thing to come in. There was no food in the house anyway, and it was already after five when I'd gotten to Burger Heaven, so the day really had been mostly mine.

First breather we get, I look around. I see Manuel's on the drive-through tonight, which means there won't be any problems there. Theresa's handling the grill. She's by herself, which means the new guy didn't show up.

Maria looks exhausted from straightening out misfilled orders and hearing complaints from people who thought their wait was too long. She's also still trying to find at least one more worker to come in for the evening shift. Being a manager is not a job I'd ever want.

Then the breather is over. Strange thing about fastfood places—the way they seem to completely empty out, and then a crowd converges all at once. At any rate, there's another rush. No more time for observations or thinking now. Just punch the orders in fast and pull them off the line as fast as the griller can get them out. The phone in the back rings, but the lines are long, and no one leaves their station to answer it. We pretend not to hear, hoping the ringing will stop. But it doesn't. Finally, Maria rushes to answer, one more duty of a manager, I guess. And I turn my attention back to the lines of burger buyers.

Suddenly, I feel a hand grab my arm. "I've got to go. It's my baby. She fell. You're in charge. Handle things," Maria says. She digs into her purse and thrusts keys into my hands. "I'll try to get back. If you have to, you can lock up tonight."

I hold the keys out for Maria to take them back from me. "I'm so sorry about your baby, I really am, but Maria, I don't, I mean I can't . . ."

And then I realize I'm talking to empty air. I stare at the keys and think of their unwanted implications. What do I know about being a manager? Nothing. What exactly is it that Maria does when she closes up?

A gum-popping guy from across the counter snorts. "Hello . . . earth to employee . . . I'd like to order . . . I mean this *is* supposed to be *fast* food, right? And it don't exactly look real fast to me."

Robotlike, I smile. "I'm so sorry for your wait. Welcome to Burger Heaven. What may I serve you today?"

SARA

Hello—out there . . . people . . . Yes. You, the ones chomping down your Blast-Off Burgers and slurping your Super Sodas. Yes, I am so talking to all of you! It is Saturday night. Did you forget? Like—what are you doing here? Do not even try to tell me that Burger Heaven is your place for weekend partying. Get out of here. And get a life!

Yeah, okay, so I don't really say all that out loud, but I sure think it. I mean, look at this place! It is so totally maxed-out. Every table is taken. I so do not believe all these dweebs waiting in lines to give their orders. You'd think they were trying to score top concert tickets instead of cheesy cheeseburgers. I mean, give me a break.

The place is already feeding time at the zoo, when a

big yellow bus pulls up and fifty more obnoxious kids pile through our door. The volume in the restaurant goes up, like, a hundred times, and I have to shout. "Your order comes to $4.72!" I tell Miss Preteen of Pimples, but she, like, has only $3.87. So her "friends" dig into their purses and pockets for more money and oh, my god, everyone behind them glares at me like it's my fault the girl didn't check before she ordered? It's, like, what do they want me to do about it?

After about a half hour, the crowd manages to find life elsewhere. Even the fifty kids from Magic-School-Bus time have found their way out of here, and the front is finally empty—*not*! I mean the mounds of paper, partially eaten burgers, stray fries, and especially the plopped ketchup designs on tables are all real clear signs that they were here. So why is it that these people cannot pick up their own garbage? Cleaning up after these zeros should so not be my job. But it's just another fantastic benefit of working for Burger Heaven.

I toss trash from the tables, mop up the ketchup messes, and try to forget I've got the next restroom check. Bathrooms at Burger Heaven are another grossosity—especially the men's. I mean what do guys do in there anyway? Like I know what they go in to do, *duh*, but why can't they do it in the toilet?

If I had just, like, one chance for a do-over, I so know what it would be. I, for sure, would not have shoplifted that red skirt. I, like, wouldn't even have cared that it fit so perfect and was going to mean all eyes on me at

Tommy R.'s party. I mean, not to exaggerate or anything, but I looked like a supermodel. With that skirt and my red heels, I was going to definitely be, like, Miss Amazing Legs.

Then I looked at the price tag. It was, like, are you kidding me? $450 for one skirt? So, like, I took the skirt off. It was so unfair.

Then I started thinking a little more. *Such a big store.* And this was, like, just one little skirt, which, I mean, I needed a lot more than they did. I mean, I for sure had a lot less cash than they did. Besides, it, like, looked so good on me that it would almost be like I was advertising for the store. I mean, they pay models to wear their stuff, right? It's not like I'm Janine, who swipes everything she ever wears. I would *so* not do that. I'm really a very honest person, but just because of Tommy R.'s party and because this skirt couldn't look so good on anyone else, I decided one little five-finger discount wouldn't hurt anyone.

Wrong. I was no more than, like, a few feet out the door into the mall when I felt this hand clamp on my arm, and I'm, like, about to say, "Take your hand off me," when this really scary voice says, "I know exactly what you've done, and you'll come with me right now."

Getting busted was like a nightmare in slow motion. I, honest to god, almost wet my pants right on the spot. They made me go back into the store and sit in this little room for a long time. They took the red skirt out of my purse and hung it on a hanger in the room. As I stared at it, I decided it really wasn't even that cute.

I, like, kept seeing myself getting sent to that awful tent city for teens doing time on weekends. So, like, after a long lecture, when they finally said something about a *second chance*, I was ready to say yes to whatever it was. And what it was was that I could get off with a warning if I'd get a job, pay back double damages, and keep myself out of trouble.

Okay, I admit it. I was relieved. I mean, I wasn't going to that tent-city place. I could even feel myself start to breathe again. I, like, thanked them over and over, and I agreed real fast to find a "court-approved" job right away and keep it for my whole probation. But I am so sure that I didn't really get it then that I'd be spending all my Saturday nights ringing up burgers and cleaning up after slobs.

It's all so totally unfair. Janine still steals stuff all the time, and she's never gotten caught even once. But me— I get busted my very first time! I didn't even get to go to Tommy R.'s party, and now, I barely even remember what the skirt looked like. Instead, I see the disgusting men's bathroom. But wait a minute—with Maria being gone, just what's Jordan going to do if I say I'm not cleaning those repulsive restrooms tonight? I mean, Jordan's no more a manager than me, right?

THERESA

I am feeling great as I jump into the shower. Desert Shadow High put an all-weather track in last year, and I try get there on Saturdays whenever I can. This track is so much easier on my knees than our old gravel one. This morning, I actually got a chance to jog for over an hour, and that always clears my head. When I got done, I stretched, and then I came home in time to do my full Pilates workout.

I love these Saturdays when I have a later shift at Burger Heaven. I know that Mom isn't so thrilled to have me on until ten at night, but it's so worth it to have the morning to myself to work out. I pull on my Burger Heaven uniform, leave Mom a note telling her that maybe we'll watch a movie on TV when we both get home, and I head for BH.

As I walk, I think about the shift chart I checked yesterday. I'm supposed to be on with some new guy today. Bad news is that this will be the new guy's first shift, and I'll probably have to explain how everything works.

In the back, except for me, it's pretty much of a revolving door. Why I don't know. It's so dumb, because employees get bonuses and pay raises the longer they stick around. A couple of weeks ago, a new guy said he used to work at Taco Bell, but he skipped two shifts because he wanted to go on a road trip with his buddies. Then he decided that since he hadn't called in, Taco Bell would probably fire him, so he just didn't go back. Of course, he only showed up here for a week, and then we never saw him again either.

When I get in today, Juan is just about to leave. He nods, says "*Hola,*" and that's about our entire conversation before his shift ends. Forty minutes later, it's pretty obvious that the new guy is going to be a no-show. Maria sighs and says she'll work on getting a replacement before the dinner rush. She says he's not the only no-show for the afternoon, and she heads to the office to start making calls. I don't envy her. It's not going to be easy finding someone who hasn't already made plans by this time on a Saturday.

The afternoon is fairly slow, and I don't think much more about it, until it suddenly gets real crowded up front. The orders start pouring in, and even though I work fast, I'm way backed up. I'm flipping ten burgers at once, thinking we really need that second person, and hoping Maria got hold of someone. I toss the burgers onto the buns, and then the next batch of orders blows in.

Suddenly, I look up and I can't believe what I see. Alex is strutting through the door like he owns the place. He starts for the back, sees me, stops a minute, and smirks. He swaggers on toward the grill, but before he can say or do anything else, I wave my greasy spatula at him, and I tell the skunk that he can just slink his sorry self right back out of here. I remind him that he isn't allowed to be on the premises when I'm working, and just in case he can't read, my name is on the schedule for tonight.

Alex folds his arms across his chest. "They asked me to work tonight. I had to leave two brokenhearted ladies who were hoping I'd be hanging out with them. So their loss is Burger Heaven's gain. I'm here, and I'm staying!"

I don't mind working hard, but a deal is a deal. And that deal says Alex is not supposed to be on my shifts. I storm out front to find Maria. How could she have forgotten! If she is letting him stay, I am signing myself out for the night, and they can just pay me for it anyway!

It's weird but when I get out front, I don't see Maria anywhere. I ask Jordan, who's trying to work two registers at once. Between orders, she says something about an emergency, and she wishes she weren't, but she's in charge until Maria comes back.

"Emergency? But what—," I start to say.

"Excuse me," this beer-bellied guy interrupts, "but I've been waiting for ten minutes, and I still don't have my order. Can I just get my money back?"

Jordan apologizes and tries to explain that we're a little shorthanded. The guy doesn't care. His voice gets louder. He has places to be. There's an ASU game on TV tonight!

Just then, Alex gets the order out. Jordan grabs it, gives it to the guy, and refunds his money. "This is complimentary. We're sorry it took a little longer. Burger Heaven prides itself on its service. And . . . and I hope the Sun Devils win tonight."

Then she turns to me, on the edge of tears. "Theresa, I'm really sorry. I know you're not supposed to have to work with Alex. I wasn't supposed to be here either, and I sure don't know anything about being a manager. All I know is that with Maria gone, we're short three people, and look at this place! If you leave, how will I ever handle tonight? Please, is there any way you could just stay until Maria gets back?"

I think for a minute. Jordan's got no more power than me. And I suppose I can take care of myself where Alex is concerned. After all, I was only eight when I stood up to my stepdad.

I can still see Mom's black eyes and remember her bruises from the jerk's beatings. But in spite of everything awful that man did to her, Mom always gave him another chance. Or two. Or ten. She was too scared to break free. At nine, I was the one who insisted we sneak out of the house before he came home that night, and I was the one telling my mom we would survive living in a shelter. I was the one who wouldn't let us turn back.

Not to say that it wasn't rough. We had meals at the Salvation Army, and there were nights when we weren't sure where we would sleep, but it was still better than being in that house with him.

Me and Mom, we're doing okay now. It's just that everything costs so much. It's always a struggle. But I'm not really complaining. My mom could have left me and gone off to have an easier life. She wouldn't have been the first mother in my old neighborhood to do such a thing. But my mom has always tried to take care of me. She has always loved me.

"Uh, Theresa, please?" Jordan says, and I realize I've been standing in the middle of all this chaos thinking. Jordan needs me tonight. And why should I let that Alex creep cut short the money I bring home? I can take care of myself.

"I'll finish my shift," I tell Jordan. "So don't worry." I march back to the grill. I'll tell Alex tonight's rules, and if he gets out of line, I know hamburgers are not the only things that can get grilled.

ALEX

Haven't said or done anything, but Theresa's already in my face with a greasy grill turner, yapping about rules. Yeah, well I got a few rules, too.

#1 I'm not desperate.

#2 I'm not stupid.

#3 I'm not messing with her—no more—no way!

Fact is, she's just pissed because she wants me, and she doesn't want to want me. Well, too late for her. She'll be sorry, though. When I'm the big star, she'll be begging, "Remember me?"

"Theresa, who?" I'll say. "Nope. Don't know her."

Of course, I might be doing some looking tonight. No rules against enjoying a little eye candy, right?

MRS. WILKINS

My daughter doesn't have to know everything I do. I don't remember asking her to be in charge of me. How could I have produced such a worrywart? I'm sure I was not that overprotective of her when she was young.

I try to tell Ann I love her, and I appreciate her concern, but truly, I can take good care of myself. And besides, she already has quite enough to do. She is an attorney, a mother, and a community activist. My gracious, even for Ann, that should be more than enough.

But, I am sorry to say, she now sees me as another project that she must handle with her usual logical efficiency. In fact, I wouldn't be surprised if scheduled into that BlackBerry-thing she always has with her is an ongoing reminder to worry about Mom. She means well, she does, and I love her dearly. But her decrees are driving me crazy.

I must carry a cell phone, she says. "But who do I need to call?" I ask. "For my entire life, I've done just fine without a cellular phone."

Two days later, Ann arrives with the phone she's purchased for me. She patiently explains lots of features I'll never use, nor remember, but I listen. And because it makes her happy, I carry the phone she has given me. No one ever calls me on it, but I carry it whenever I go out.

Ann also says that I must cease driving at night. She's afraid I might not see well enough after dark. I inform her that is absolute hogwash! I'm not making cross-country trips. In fact, my usual nighttime destination is only Burger Heaven, a short, right-turn-only route that I could do in my sleep.

And that brings up her next decree. I must cease eating at Burger Heaven. She's afraid I might raise my cholesterol level. I tell her, "Absurd! I've lived to eighty-six. What difference will a few more hamburgers make?" Then she gets all upset, and she tells me I must not talk like that.

I really do not wish to be difficult. I simply want to live my own life as I see fit. However, it seems that to do so, I have to sneak out, as if I'm sixteen again. It's absolutely preposterous, I know, but each time, I hope I'll get to Burger Heaven and home without getting caught by Ann.

I especially enjoy my visits when a nice young man named Manuel waits on me.

He always remembers my order, and sometimes he even treats me to an apple pie.

If it's not too busy, he tells me about school. How nice it is to be involved in that world again. After more than thirty-five years as a teacher and counselor, I think high school will always be a part of me, and I know that Manuel is a young man who could have a stellar future. He just needs some encouragement about going to college.

Often, at Burger Heaven, I enjoy taking my hamburger and sitting at the picnic tables by the slides. Watching frazzled parents trying to tire their tots for bed, the years fall away, and I remember our many excursions to the park so very long ago, when Ann was small.

Sometimes, if the Burger Heaven playground is deserted, I sit inside in a bright-green booth and eavesdrop on the beginnings of budding romance, tearful talk, or shared gossip.

Why can't my daughter understand that this place is good for me? I realize that she's way too busy to have Mom in the middle of her everyday life, and I wouldn't want her to feel guilty about that. But I am just not ready to be put on a shelf like some fragile, breakable vase, so I'll always be safe and available. That is simply no kind of life for a person. No matter how many times Ann and I discuss the matter, she just can't see that coming to Burger Heaven a few evenings a week is so much better than facing four lonely walls. I treasure my independence in choosing when I will come and then driving myself here.

Sometimes, as I sit in my booth, I raise my strawberry shake in a silent toast to all the phantom friends who've passed away, and to the ever-changing collage of interesting people that sitting at Burger Heaven allows me to know.

MANUEL

I was trying to help Jordan cover one cash register and work the drive-through at the same time. And if I had had an extra pair of arms and legs, I could have used them, too. It can be a killer when we're slammed with business and short on employees. All that's ended for now. In fact, the place is completely and totally empty, but my brain and my body still think they should be going ninety miles an hour. It's really hard to slow down.

Bored, I turn to watch the scene in the back. Theresa and Alex move cautiously in the kitchen area. The deep freeze is obvious to everyone.

I'm sorry I wasn't here to actually see the Ketchup Incident, as it's been named by everyone who saw it. It's become a kind of Burger Heaven legend. And though a rematch would be something to see, I'm glad that no one is throwing anything at anyone tonight. Jordan seems stressed out enough without having to handle another battle between Theresa and Alex, which, despite Alex's muscles, I'd still bet on Theresa to win.

From the corner of my eye, I see the light on the soft-serve machine is blinking, which means that it needs to be refilled with mix. I used to really like soft-serve ice-cream cones, but since I've had to clean the machine a thousand times, I'm not so crazy about them anymore. I drain the last of the mix, which comes out a little like glue, clean the spigot, and pour more Lowfat Tasty Chocolate Soft Serve into the top of the machine.

Yawning, I stare at the clock. It seems as if the minutes barely move. I'd rather work when it's too busy than too quiet. But the restaurant remains empty. It's not my job tonight, but I'm thinking about getting a rag to wipe down the booths just for something to do, when finally, I see a car's headlights turning in to the parking lot. Ahhh . . . it's Mrs. Wilkins. Too bad I can't conjure up a crowd for her to have around. She so enjoys the people. She enters the store. I see the disappointment cross her face as she notes how empty it is. She walks up to the counter, smiling broadly when she sees me.

"Manuel, I was hoping you would be working tonight!" Digging deep into her big old-fashioned black handbag, she continues, "Remember what we were talking about? Well, I called Scottsdale Community College and Paradise Valley Community College, too. I got all this information for you. Oh, and I learned that Burger Heaven even offers some employee scholarships. I'll bet we could get you one of them."

Sweet old lady is losing it. That's what I thought when Mrs. Wilkins first mentioned me and college in the same sentence. I mean, the guys make fun of me for thinking I'm even going to get my own truck. I can just imagine what they'd say about this. *Manuel* and *college* are just not two words that anyone other than Mrs. Wilkins has ever put together.

It's weird, though. I mean, a couple of weeks ago, my English teacher did say my writing was interesting and showed maturity. Then, the other day, my Algebra teacher called me *astute*, which I think is a good thing. And I don't know why I did it, but one night after Mrs. Wilkins had been giving me another of her pep talks, I mentioned college to my mom, thinking she'd put the idea out of my head immediately, but Mama didn't laugh or tell me that I was being foolish. Instead, her eyes started to shine, and she said, "First you, and then maybe Mayra and Miguel."

Tonight, Mrs. Wilkins presses the information from the community colleges into my hand. She says, "I used to help lots of students fill out applications. I could wait until you are on break, and then I could help you with this."

I'm actually considering Mrs. Wilkins's offer, when I

realize that Jordan is right behind me wiping down the counter, and she has to have overheard this conversation. My face is on fire. I'm sure she's laughing at me because I don't realize college is a place for the Jordans of the world, not the Manuels. I hear her name on the announcements at Desert Shadow all the time for one more award that she's won. But I'm sure she doesn't even know I go to the same school.

"Thanks, but I really don't think I'll need these," I say, handing the materials back to Mrs. Wilkins. "I'll have your order up fast—the usual, right?"

"But Manuel," Mrs. Wilkins starts to say. And she's a really sweet old lady who's only trying to be nice, so I hate to cut her off. But I do, because I may not be college material, but I do have my pride.

"Excuse me, Mrs. Wilkins, I've got to check on your burger. I'm not sure the order was entered right."

Jordan looks at me strangely and then says, "Uh, Manuel, according to the chart, it is now time for your break. Why don't you go ahead, and I'll finish up this order."

Now, we both know that there's no such thing as a break chart. What's she up to? "Okay . . . but . . . the drive-through . . ." I say, trying to think of any excuse.

"It's pretty quiet. I think I can handle it," Jordan replies. "Give me your headphone, and take your break."

What choice do I have? As I hand her my headphone, she whispers, "Go for it!"

I am so surprised.

"Thanks," I say. I take a deep breath, and I can hardly believe it's me when I say, "Well, Mrs. Wilkins, I guess I do have a break after all. Could I treat you to an apple pie while we talk about college?"

Mrs. Wilkins smiles. "Why, that would be lovely."

JORDAN

It's getting near closing time, and I might as well admit it. Maria isn't coming back. Her daughter must be in bad shape. I'm sure she's got bigger things to worry about than Burger Heaven, and I know she needs this job. If I can get the place closed okay, maybe the big management won't even have to know she left without following procedures, and she won't get fired. I think about how much Maria talks about her daughter, and how hard it must be for her to be a single mother.

I tell myself that I can figure out how to close for Maria. After all, it can't possibly be as hard as one of Mrs. P.'s calculus problems. I think I remember hearing that there's a Burger Heaven manual in the back office. With any luck, it will give clear closing instructions. At least I already know the responsibilities the front-end employees have.

And that means I have to get Sara going on cleaning the restrooms. Some nights, I think it's pretty funny to listen to her excuses to the manager on duty, but tonight that's me, and I could use her cooperation. No need to worry about Manuel; he'll do whatever is needed, and he'll do it fast. Might as well let him talk to Mrs. Wilkins for a little longer.

I walk back to the office, which is a complete mess. For a minute, I think it's kind of funny that they're always telling us to keep the kitchen, the restrooms, and the front area spotless. They sure don't listen to their own good advice. Then, under a stack of papers on the left corner of the desk, I see a big black notebook with a label running down the side: BURGER HEAVEN POLICIES AND PROCEDURES.

I open it to find random pages stuck in everywhere. Let's see . . .

CHANGING THE FRYER OIL,

CASHING OUT,

UNDERGOING HEALTH INSPECTION,

USING THE PANIC BUTTON.

Well, that's weird. I don't think anyone ever mentioned anything about a panic button in this place. Maybe that's only for Burger Heavens in high-crime areas. I leaf through more pages. Somewhere in here, there's got to be information on closing the place for the night. Ah, finally, the right section. I skim it quickly and then reread it. Actually, it doesn't look all that hard. I can get this done for Maria. Just a little longer, and I can go home and back to bed.

PLANS

DONE AND UNDONE

DYLAN

I peel past my old high school and smirk at the cage that honestly thought its iron fence could contain me. A PE class is running laps. What simpletons—a word most of them couldn't understand, even though they are its perfect definition in their brainless blue uniforms. What could I possibly have had in common with such people?

Did Carter High's toothless teachers and powerless principal really believe they could control me? "You're so smart, Dylan," they said. "You're not applying yourself," they said. "You cannot keep breaking the rules," they said. Well, they were right about some of it. I am extremely smart.

I knew that even before Mr. Gregory showed me my

IQ score. He acted as if I should be quite honored when he informed me that he wasn't supposed to share this information, but he felt that if I understood my potential, I might better understand my obligation to live up to it. Mr. Gregory said, "Your IQ means you border on being an absolute genius, so why are you failing my history class?"

With the same smirk that frequently garnered me an invitation to detention, I answered, "'Every conquered people should have a revolt.' A quote by a famous French general—ah, wait, we haven't talked about him yet in History. But you must know who I mean." Then, just to further illustrate my point, I struck Napoleon's well-known pose—except I extended my middle finger.

However, that was not the reason that Carter High finally agreed with my assessment of the absurdity of my being there. In a rather great irony, those who thought they were in power complained that I was not applying myself and then became quite disturbed when I did so, even though I believe my application was rather restrained.

I simply felt the necessity to assist a friend of mine with a decision he had to make, so I brought a .22 to school. No one seemed the least bit reassured when I explained it wasn't as if I was carrying a Glock, clearly the weapon of choice for a serious confrontation. Thus Carter High and I parted ways, which was really no great loss for either of us.

JOE

If I'd just been absent during English, would I ever have been in such a mess? It all started with Miss Novack's assignment called "Apply Poetry to Life." I don't know why, but she always gives our assignments stupid titles. Anyway, for this one, she said we had to pick a classmate's name from a hat and then write an illustrated simile that captured who the person is.

She interrupted herself to remind us that a simile is a comparison that uses *like* or *as*, which I don't think anyone remembered. "When you think of your simile for your classmate, do not, I repeat, *do not* just pick something from the top of your head. Spend some time thinking about the person, and then in just a few words, reveal who he or she really is by your selection of a great comparison."

Lucky for me, I drew Jeff's name. He's our class comic, and everyone loves his sense of humor. I didn't even have to think what to write. "Jeff, like a well-told joke, leaves people with a lasting smile." It was going to be an easy A. Much easier than for whoever drew my name. I had no idea what they'd say about me, because I had no idea what I'd say about myself.

The next day, we turned the similes in, and I thought that was the end of it. But no, all of a sudden, Miss Novack announced that she planned to read every simile aloud.

> Linda, like a fire engine, readily rushes to help those in need.
> James, like a jaguar, pounces on opposing linemen.
> Lori, like a puzzle box, is filled with secrets within secrets.
> Josh, like a firecracker, is explosive but not dangerous unless you come too close.
> Meghan, like a flag, is always ready to wave at guys.

The weird thing was that as Miss Novack read, people actually stopped sleeping or texting or daydreaming. I mean, everyone was into it, laughing, making comments, even applauding some of the similes. We'd known each other for a million years, or at least since we'd been five.

Maybe that's why all the descriptions were so dead on. I'd never really thought about it, but a puzzle box was a good comparison for Lori. As long as I'd known her, I'd never been able to tell what she really thought. And Josh, well . . . a firecracker was a great simile for him. I kept my distance for just that reason.

The bell rang before they got to me. I wondered if mine would be as good as the ones I'd heard today.

Then I sort of forgot about it. After all, it was just English. The next day, Miss Novack had almost finished with all the similes, and it was dumb but I was beginning to get a little nervous. Then she read, "Joe is like a white wall, still too uncertain for any flash of color."

"That's good," "Great simile!" came two voices from behind me.

"Yeah, that's exactly the way Joe is!" said another voice, and then the class continued. But I didn't. I kept hearing that comparison again and again, and everyone seeing me in just that way.

All the other kids in the class had been *something* . . . a firecracker, a lion, a wishing well, a computer, a planet. But me . . . I was nothing—only a white wall, a person who was boring, unnoticed, and dull. Who'd want to be around someone like that? The more I thought about it, the more the words stung—because they were so true. And whose fault was that? Mine.

I told myself that before the day was over, I'd show everyone that the simile was wrong. I wasn't that blank person. I would do something to put a slash of color on my white wall. I felt better as soon as I made the decision. However, class after class slipped away, and I remained in my usual nobody state.

Then it was seventh-hour chem lab, the last class of the day, and I was paired with Alicia. She had transferred here just two weeks ago, and her Southern drawl and deep dimples had made a big impression.

We went to lab station fourteen. Alicia poured a mixture into a beaker and handed it to me. I held the beaker over the Bunsen burner, and while waiting for it to heat, I told myself this was it. It was the last chance to do something besides be a blank wall.

Taking a deep breath, I forced myself to say, "So, maybe I'll come over to your house this weekend." I was gulping on the inside, but miraculously, my voice didn't even crack.

Even more of a miracle, Alicia didn't shoot me down. She only asked, "Oh yeah, how come?" accompanied by a smile that actually might indicate interest. My heart was pounding so hard, I almost dropped the beaker, especially when I realized I hadn't thought things out enough for any kind of a good answer. But Alicia was waiting, hands on her hips, eyes on me.

Who knows where it came from, but I heard my voice saying, "Oh, I just thought I'd show you my new truck."

"Hmmm." She smiled again. "New truck—nice—tell me about it?"

So I did. I described the truck in great detail. I even explained about its mag wheels. "Sounds pretty special.

Can't wait to see it." Then Alicia actually gave me her address. I walked out of Chemistry knowing that in my hand, I had a really hot girl's address, and she actually wanted me to come over to her house. Hey, I didn't care whether it was because she wanted to see me or my truck. Any way I looked at it, I was a happy man. No more white-wall Joe!

In fact, I didn't just leave school that Friday, I strutted out like some kind of proud peacock in full color! Now, there was a better simile for the new me. As I started home, I couldn't stop grinning. Who could have guessed it was so easy to get invited to a great-looking girl's house? If I'd known it was that simple, I would definitely have tried it before.

I walked a couple of blocks feeling fantastic, until I came back to earth enough to realize what I had actually done. It was my mouth talking without my brain thinking, because the truck—the new one I was supposed to drive up to Alicia's in—wasn't mine. I'd described every detail because that truck was all my older cousin Jesse had talked about for years before he'd finally saved enough money to get it. I'd gone with him to Ernhardt Ford a couple of times to visit his truck before he'd gotten it, but since he'd gotten it home, I hadn't even been invited for a ride. In fact, he wouldn't even let me touch the steering wheel because he didn't want my fingerprints on it. So how was I ever going to get him to let me drive that truck away? The answer was simple: I wasn't.

Good-bye, Alicia. Hello, Joe, the white wall.

DYLAN

Carter High was worried that I wouldn't use my brain if I left their inane attempts at instruction. How surprised would they be to know that I've analyzed Machiavelli, Patton, and other great thinkers?

However, I don't plan to spend my life reading about others. In fact, I regard myself as an entrepreneur, with strategies to become extremely wealthy. Of course, I will have to do so entirely on my own. Unlike those kids with CEOs for parents, I have no affluent father or moneyed mother to hand me the keys to success. My mom frets about my future from the lofty depths of her two-bit waitressing job at Denny's, and my dad is a poor slob who spends his life glued to the seat of a truck making short-run deliveries. He thought I should stay in school to get ahead; I paid as much attention to that advice as I did to everything else he ever told me. I'm not certain how it was genetically possible for two such people as they to have sired me, but at least they have learned to leave me alone. I come and go as I wish. No questions allowed. Still, I choose not to remain in their house for much longer.

I have developed a sound business plan for myself. Unfortunately, I lack the initial capital for my economic base. I have no doubt that I can maximize my money a hundred times over, but first I need sufficient start-up funding. That means, for the time being, I live at home, and for the time being, these robberies are essential. I certainly do not regard myself as some type of petty thief; that would be beneath me. These robberies are only a temporary means to a greater end.

Without any conceit, I can honestly say that the reason the thefts have worked so well is because it is my mind that is planning them. Certainly, Greg knows that. It is why he follows my rules precisely, and it is precisely the reason that money flows into his pockets. Granted, I would prefer to conduct these operations by myself, but my plan necessitates two people for maximum gain with minimum risk. Thus, Greg. And yes, I studied carefully before selecting him. For a time, I frequented a particular pool hall, and I struck up games and conversations with many until I was certain that Greg was my man. He was the perfect combination of dumb, greedy, and loyal.

Five times now we've struck. We are quite efficient in getting the cash. And not that I care about such things, but really, who have these robberies harmed? Not the employees. They don't get hurt, and after it's over, they have something exciting to reveal in their usually mundane lives. Not the store. They get a windfall of free advertising. Their location and product name is shown on every TV news channel. How much would that cost normally? Certainly far more than the money they lose from a night's robbery. They ought to be thanking me for selecting their establishment to rob.

So far, our esteemed police force has not one single lead about the Ski Mask Bandits. On television they showed a sketch from an alleged eyewitness. It was of a face obliterated by a black mask that could have been any human being. One officer was interviewed saying that they were examining the crooks' pattern. I laughed. The pattern is that we don't use a pattern. And it has worked brilliantly. Each robbery has been different enough to prevent detection, and after this one, there will be no more. So let the police keep searching. There's little challenge left in this game.

This last infusion of cash should be enough for the next stage in my wealth-accumulation plan. I've sufficiently researched, and cultivated my new business contacts, and finally, they trust me enough to let me make a big buy. I've worked out my own distribution system, a kind of private drugstore, if you will, with me being my own CEO.

Greg doesn't know this is the last occasion of our partnership, but he does understand the pre-robbery routine. The week before a hit, he makes certain that he stays out of trouble and lays low.

"Where we going this time?" Greg always asks.

"Can't say."

"How do you know it'll have money?" Greg always asks.

"Haven't they all?" I never tell him much. He does his job well, and that's as much as he needs to know. He has no idea of the effort that goes into my planning. But it is well worth my time for, as Patton inelegantly put it, "A pint of sweat saves a gallon of blood." And my robberies are meant to be bloodless. Sometimes, it takes weeks of research and surveillance and even sweat to select the ideal spot. However, finding this location was almost embarrassingly easy.

Some big breasts without much brain babbled on at a kegger about how she wished we could go out, but it couldn't be on a weekend because she always had to work at this Burger Heaven. She said I wouldn't believe how much cash they kept around on weekends because the place was too cheap to pay for overtime security pickup. Now, I know better than to believe anyone, especially some boozed-out bimbo, so I verified every detail. I made myself a Burger Heaven customer, coming at very busy times so I could observe what went on without being remembered. I examined the layout of the restaurant and watched the workers.

That was only the beginning. I'm far more thorough than that, for there is absolutely no point in conducting a robbery if the amount of money on the premises is insufficient. Thus, I made sure to have coffee with a security driver who picked up from that Burger Heaven on Monday mornings. Unobtrusively, I followed the driver for a week before I casually walked into a doughnut place far from Burger Heaven, where he had stopped for coffee.

I had watched the driver massage his back each time he got in and out of his truck, so as I sat down at the counter next to him, I groaned and held my back. It was he who initiated the conversation. I knew he would. We talked about aching backs, and it was easy for me to steer the conversation to job-related strains on the back. It was the driver who actually volunteered the complaint that Burger Heaven's Saturday deposit was the bag that was so heavy it was killing him.

My role was simply to be a good listener. "Must take in a lot of cash on Saturdays," I said.

"Yep, too cheap to pay for a weekend pickup," he explained. Then we went on to talk of other things. Days later, would he remember me or this idle conversation we had? Of course not.

The important point was that the party girl was right. Burger Heaven was ripe to be robbed on a Saturday night. A lesser person would never have picked up on the clues. A lesser person would never have been able to confirm that this fast-food restaurant with so little security and so much cash was just calling out to come and remove it. Fortunately, I am definitely not a lesser person.

JOE

I make up my mind to stop by Jesse's on the way home, because I will not let myself just give up and fade back into that blank wall. As I walk, I keep thinking, *Is there anything in the whole world that I've got that Jesse wants enough to lend me his truck?* But as hard as I think, I keep coming up with only one answer—*No.*

Okay, so with that answer, where am I? Zeroed out. I almost turn around to go home, but then I start telling myself that Jesse has had the truck for almost two months. Maybe he's ready to let someone else see what it drives like. Maybe he'd like to show it off that way. Maybe he's not even still polishing it every day.

When I get to Jesse's, I don't see him outside working

on his truck, which would be a good sign, but then again, I don't see his truck, either. I hope he's just got it in the garage.

I ring the bell, and my cousin Suzi answers the door. "Haven't seen you in a couple of weeks. What's up?"

We talk for a minute before I casually ask, "Jesse around?"

She tells me that he's working late tonight. "With those big payments on that truck of his, he gets in the extra hours when he can. Did you need him for anything special?"

"Not really . . . is he going to be around tomorrow?"

Suzi shrugs. "He's got the day off work, but who knows."

I'd like to ask her what would impress a girl like Alicia, but I don't. And besides, what difference does it make if I can't get the truck. "Well, tell him . . . tell him, I'm gonna stop by tomorrow morning."

Friday night crawls by. The minutes on the clock almost forget to move. At dinner, Mom asks me how my day was, and I shrug. "About like usual," I answer. I play computer games for the rest of the night, but my scores are awful. I can't concentrate.

Finally, Saturday morning comes. I don't have to worry about waking up too late. I haven't been able to sleep. Tell me how dumb this is, but I get up, walk over to Jesse's, and wait outside. I don't want to wake him up if he's sleeping in, because that will really tick him off, and I don't want him to leave before I get there, so I just wait.

Finally, I see the garage door go up. "Hey, Jesse," I call as I get closer, and I hope he can't hear the nerves I feel.

"Hey, Joe!" Jesse seems glad enough to have me around. He says I can help him wash the truck. It's already so shiny that it gleams, but I say, "Sure." We talk as we wash, but nothing about me borrowing his truck. Finally, I say, "Hey, Jesse, you know that I've had my license for almost four months now."

In some fantasy world, this would be the time that he would reply, "Four months, huh, and I bet you haven't even had a decent set of wheels to try out." Then I'd say that I hadn't, and Jesse would say, "Well, why don't you try taking my truck so you can see how the best drives." And I'd say that sounded great, and it would be done.

But who am I kidding? Jesse doesn't say anything at all like that. In fact, he doesn't say anything about my license; he just starts talking about the torque of the engine. The truck is even more spotless, if that's possible, than it was before we washed it. Jesse looks pleased. "It's a beauty, isn't it?"

Old white-wall Joe is about to give up and go home, when my brain sees Alicia's dimpled smile, and I take a deep breath. Hinting is not going to work. I've got to be blunt.

I blurt, "Jesse, is there any way I could borrow your truck tonight, or if you've got a date, how about tomorrow afternoon?"

Jesse laughs. "That's a good one, little cuz. You taking my truck? Funniest joke of the day."

"It's no joke." I can hear the desperation in my voice.

I guess Jesse hears it too. He actually stops polishing and says, "It's a girl, right?"

I nod, and he says, "Man, looks like you got it bad. Hey, I wish you luck with your lady, but my truck stays with me."

At this point, I have nothing left to lose by begging. "Jesse, please, I'll be so careful. Your truck will still be perfect when I bring it back; I'll fill it up with gas even if it's on empty when you give it to me. And afterwards . . . I'll . . . I'll even come and I'll wash it every weekend for a month."

Jesse punches me in the arm. "She must be some girl. Reminds me of the thing I had for Stephanie."

I remember that! Jesse had such a crush on her. I hope maybe he's thinking about what that felt like, and that's making him reconsider a little. I just have to come up with the right words to push it over. "Hey, Jesse, isn't there anything you want as much as I want to borrow your truck?"

He laughs and polishes out another imaginary spot. "Are you kidding?"

But I can't let it go. "Really . . . if you could have anything you don't have right now, what would it be?"

Jesse finally puts down his rag and thinks. Then he looks at me. "Crash is in concert tomorrow night. I guess if I could have anything besides my truck, it would be a Crash ticket right down in front, but . . . I don't exactly have any extra cash for concert tickets."

Now, I know all about Crash. They're Jesse's favorite

band. He's downloaded every song they've ever made. They've never been in Phoenix before, and even though Dodge Theatre is big, their concert has been sold out for weeks. "So . . . what if I get you a Crash ticket?"

"I don't see any way you can do it, but little cuz, you bring me a ticket, for the main floor first fifteen rows, and the truck is yours to borrow for a few hours."

I give Jesse a high five. I tell him to count on going to that concert. He grins and we shake on the deal. However, he adds that I shouldn't count on the truck. I'll never be able to get those tickets.

"But a deal is a deal, right?" I say.

Jesse shakes his head. "She must be some girl. I told you Crash tickets aren't still around, but sure, it's a deal."

"Okay," I reply. "Then count on a ticket and count on me taking your truck."

As I leave, Jesse is laughing, and I'm pretty sure he's laughing at me. But I don't care. He may not think I'll be back with that ticket, but I will, and one thing about Jesse—he does always keep his word. That's just the way he is.

Man, I am so glad that I didn't give up. Everything is going to be perfect. Jesse's going to love the concert. Then, after he sees how I treat his truck, and I offer to pay for gas, he may even let me start borrowing it regularly. And Alicia . . . well maybe I'm going to have a good reason to use that truck all the time!

I close my eyes and actually see myself pulling up in front of Alicia's house in Jesse's gleaming blue truck, and for the first time I know that boring white-wall Joe will be living life in bright, beautiful color.

I can't wait to get home and get on the Internet for scalper tickets to Crash. I figure I'm going to have to pay way above the fifty-dollar ticket price for the main floor, but hey, that's okay. I've got money saved, and borrowing the truck will be worth it, even if I have to pay double for Crash tickets.

I log on to the computer. It says that Dodge Theatre has five thousand seats and they're all sold out for this concert. But that's okay. I get out of the official site, and sure enough, there are sellers! There'd have to be with that many seats. I click on the first, then the second, and third, and I can't believe it . . . they actually want seven hundred dollars minimum per Crash ticket on the main floor near the front. Great . . . even after I've dug out all the cash I have, I'm still $456.82 short.

$456.82. How am I ever going to get so much money so fast? Maybe I could get a job. Is there any one-day job that pays that much? Probably not. Even if there is, why would they hire me? All I've ever done for pay is mow lawns and pick weeds. Not exactly the kind of work experience to get big bucks fast.

Maybe I could borrow the money. But no one I know has that kind of cash. So who does have money? Banks. Maybe I could rob a bank. Very funny.

Meanwhile, as I'm trying to think, I'm watching the computer screen, and people are actually buying Crash tickets even at that crazy price. I can't stand it. I turn off the computer. Sometimes, I think better when I walk, so I grab some Gatorade and take off. I walk and walk, hoping I'll come up with something. I keep wishing that I'd never heard of that dumb English assignment. And I keep wishing that Alicia hadn't seemed almost interested in me. Most of all, I keep wishing that I had some way to get over four hundred dollars fast.

My feet pound the pavement, and in frustration of not even one good idea, I begin to jog a little faster. When I finally glance at a street sign, I realize I'm miles from my house. I look at my watch. I might as well admit defeat and go home. As I wait to cross the street to head back, I see some homeless guy standing on the median holding one of those hand-lettered cardboard signs. I think, *Well, I guess I could be worse off. He may need it, but he's sure not going to get any money that way.* But as I'm waiting for the light, I see the homeless guy pocketing bills from guilty arms and manicured hands that roll down windows, extend cash, and retreat into their fancy cars.

The light changes; I could walk across the street, but I don't. I stand watching as the light turns from red to green several times. Each time, the guy pockets more money. I start to wonder . . . No . . . it's crazy . . . no way . . . how could I even think about doing it? Me—who has a nice, average home and enough clothes and food to eat.

And me, who has absolutely no way to get $456.82 fast.

KEITH

Miss Simcor is my nicest teacher. I been in her class all four years—for special resource. She told me, "Happy birthday, Keith." She said it right when I came to her class. She told me, "I know it's not until tomorrow, but since tomorrow is Saturday, I wanted to tell you today."

Miss Simcor is smart. She remembers everything. Miss Simcor said I was growed up. She was proud of how much I had growed up in three years. She said I should be proud because I was going to graduate this year.

I told her I didn't want to be growed up. I told her I wanted to come back next year. I told her I still wanted to be in her class. She smiled. She said I would be fine without her. She said I had lots more adventures to go do. I don't know about that. Miss Simcor's room is my safe place at school. I'll be sad if I can't come to Miss Simcor's class.

I walked home from school today. I walk home every day, but today, I thought about my birthday. I hope my mom will remember. Sometimes, she forgets. Sometimes, she is very busy.

I got home today. Mom wasn't there. But there was an envelope on the kitchen table. It said, "To Keith." I was happy. I knew what it was. It was a birthday card. My mom didn't forget this time!

It wasn't my birthday until tomorrow, but I wanted to open the card now. I wanted Mom to hurry up and come home. Then I could ask her if I could open my card now.

I waited. It got dark. Mom didn't come home. I was sad. I watched TV, and I looked at my card. But I guess I fell asleep. It was morning. I was still in my clothes. I was still on the sofa. The TV was still on. And my mom still wasn't home.

Mom? Where are you?

DYLAN

I stop by the pigsty that Greg calls home, just to review his part in my plan for tonight. He's too stupid to earn much money on his own, but he has done a fine job of following my specific directions at each robbery, and that is all he has to do. If I had selected a partner who thought he was as smart as I, not only would he have been wrong, but he might make the mistake of thinking he's the one in control and get us both in trouble. Greg is, as I knew he would be, the perfect accomplice.

I detest coming to his apartment, climbing the stairs, stepping over the trash, and trying not to let the odor of the halls assault my nose. The doorbell is still broken, so I knock on his flimsy door, which feels as if it were made of cardboard. There's no answer. I knock louder. I'm starting to get mildly irritated. Greg had better not be drunk! He knows I won't tolerate that before a job. I check my watch. There's time for me to get him sober if need be, but I'll take a portion of his money from tonight for my extra effort.

But even before I can slide my credit card in to open the lock, a little kid in the hallway says, "Ain't nobody home there; cops took those guys away."

I can feel my fury rising, but I keep my voice perfectly detached. "Is that so? Tell me about it."

"Some guy came to the door, jus' like you do now. Then the two guys got in this big ol' fight with blades and all. You jus' missed the whole thing. Cops tol' 'em they was gonna go to jail. Both of 'em." The kid is ready to continue revealing all the details, but I don't care. I have only one concern. My well-orchestrated robbery is supposed to take place tonight, and that is not going to work correctly without my partner. I bang my hand against the banister; it is so difficult to work with idiots.

Walking down the litter-filled stairwell with the kid following behind still babbling, I'm feeling rather strange; I'd say it's nerves, but I don't allow myself nervousness. I'd say it's anger, but I don't waste time on that emotion. Still, I'm immensely irritated with Greg. How dare he!

I'm thinking that, given the current circumstances, it might be better to postpone this robbery for a week or two. However, I know that is not possible. I've already committed the money from it to a midnight meeting, and I will honor that commitment tonight. But how to make it all happen?

I remember reading the inventor Charles F. Kettering, who said, "A problem well stated is a problem half solved." I clear my mind of Greg's stupidity so I can clearly delineate my current dilemma. I need a sizable amount of cash tonight, and the source for that funding is still clearly available. In fact, every detail is still in place except for my lack of an accomplice. Thus, I need only to locate one unquestioning follower within the next few hours to complete my plan.

Actually, I believe it was Goethe who said that magic is believing in yourself, and if you can do that, you can make anything happen. Thus, I have no doubt that I will find my unquestioning follower, and my life will proceed exactly as planned.

JOE

No one would believe it's me because I don't believe it myself. Not only have I never done anything like this, but I don't know anyone else who ever has, either. I am standing on a median with a sign that says *Please Help*. I made it from the back of a cardboard Pepsi box with a black crayon borrowed from the homeless guy. He lent me the crayon because I promised to stay away from his spot. My median is about a ten-minute walk farther down the street from him and that much farther from my house.

Cars begin to zip by me, and I hold my sign up, facing the traffic. Unbelievable. I am actually panhandling for money. At least I didn't lie. I mean, my sign doesn't say

I'm homeless or anything. And I do need help. Maybe this'll be one of those stories like my dad and his old buddies talk about after a couple of beers when they remember the good old days of high school. Until this moment, I didn't have even one crazy or wild high school story to tell. I will now.

Most drivers avoid making eye contact with me when they have to stop for the light, but some offer a buck or two. One old man gives me a five. He says something about having been hungry himself once, and I'm so embarrassed that I almost give it back, but he's driving a nice car, so I guess he's wealthy now, and he'll be okay without the five. After fifteen minutes, I have twelve bucks. That equals almost fifty dollars an hour!

I'm thinking that if I do this the whole rest of the day . . . and a lot of people stop, and there are still tickets to Crash . . . maybe . . . just maybe . . .

Then this guy not much older than me driving the greatest-looking F-150 I've ever seen pulls up right next to me, stares at me, makes a U-turn, comes around again, and stares some more. It's making me nervous, and I'm thinking maybe it's time to call it quits for this corner.

Next thing I know, his truck is parked, and he's walking up to me. It can't be that I took his spot. Look at his truck . . . he doesn't need money! As he gets closer, I think about running, but I don't because I've got a feeling I know what's happening. I'm guessing by the way he's purposely walking and looking at me that he's an undercover cop, and I am busted. What will I ever say to my parents? As soon as he gets near me, I start to explain. If I can just make him understand before he writes the ticket or gets out the handcuffs or whatever, maybe he'll let me off.

I say, "I didn't know it was illegal. I was just trying to get money for a concert ticket." He doesn't say anything, but there's something in his eyes that probably makes a lot of bad guys confess. "Uh," I say, "am I in trouble?"

"We'll see." His voice is flat. "I'll ask the questions, and you'll give the answers."

And I do. I even use "sir" as politely as I can in every answer, even though he doesn't look that much older than me. I hope he'll feel sorry for me, because right now, I'd rather be white-wall Joe than be on my way to jail.

But then, it turns out he's not a cop at all. He says he understands how much a guy needs to have a great truck to impress a girl. He tells me that girls love his F-150, and I'm right that wheels make a difference. This truck is probably the reason he's almost engaged.

We move from the middle of the median to the side of the street where he parked his truck. I don't know why, but I keep talking. I tell him all about Alicia and how hot she is. I can't tell my parents about this day, and if I tell someone from school, it could get back to Alicia, but it sure feels good to be able to tell somebody.

This guy understands perfectly. He says he used to be a lot like me, and he says he has an idea that could benefit both of us, because he needs help too. If I could give him a hand for a few minutes tonight, he'd be glad to lend me his truck for free. I can barely believe what I'm hearing. The chrome on his truck gleams. It is a hundred times better than Jesse's, and I won't have to beg or buy gas or spend all my money on a Crash ticket to borrow the F-150.

The guy, his name is Derrick, says he has his own girl problems. His girlfriend works at Burger Heaven, and he wants to propose to her there tonight. If I help him, he'll loan me his truck for all of Sunday for free!

This is great, and I tell Derrick right away that I'll help him. I'm not quite sure, though, what he needs me to do. Doesn't he have to be the one to ask his girlfriend to marry him? Derrick explains that he has this whole plan because his girlfriend wants the proposal to be a surprise and to be really unusual.

Derrick says he's thought about it a lot. And here's what he's planning. I'm supposed to pretend I'm robbing the place, and then he's coming in with a superhero mask on to "rescue" his lady. It has something to do with her favorite movie. He says he's gone to Burger Heaven when she wasn't there, and everyone who works there said they'd go along with his plan. So he is sure his girlfriend is going to be totally surprised and excited, and it's all great except his friend, who was supposed to play the robber, got the stomach flu and started puking big-time about an hour ago, and now poor Derrick is driving around bummed, thinking that even after all his plans, he might have to forget about getting engaged.

I mean, I think that's the whole story. The truth is,

once he got to the part about his truck, I started pictur-
ing myself with Alicia sitting right next to me, and I was
only sort of listening to him.

I promise to meet him a block away from the Burger
Heaven at nine fifteen tonight. Then I tell him I really
have to get home for dinner because my mom freaks if
I'm late. He kind of laughs and says that we all have to
do what we have to do.

I start to leave, and then I turn around. "Hey," I call.
"I'm counting on your truck. You sure you're going to be
there tonight?"

He grins and says, "Definitely. You can positively
count on my meeting you at nine fifteen. After all, it's
my whole future."

I figure that's true. I just want a date. I can't even
imagine what it must be like to want to get engaged. I jog
home. I have so much energy that I smile as I run. The
colors of my life are beginning to shine so bright. How
great is it that I'm going to be part of a stunt to help a guy
get engaged and that my help is going to get me some
fine-looking free wheels for a whole day to hook up with
a great-looking girl?

I remind myself that all of this has happened only because I finally took a chance and stepped out from behind my stupid white wall.

KEITH

I don't like to be home alone. I take my card, and I go to the park. I will open it there. The park is close to my house. I like the sign at the park. It says Roadrunner Park. It has a picture of a roadrunner on it. I know that it is a roadrunner. There aren't real roadrunners at the park, though.

I walk past the tennis courts. I go to the playground. I sit down. The bench is hard. I take out my birthday card. It is in a blue envelope. I open it. My card has a picture on the outside. The picture is a big trophy. It has words too. The words say *On your 18th Birthday*. There are printed words on the inside. They say *Congratulations, you're legal now*. I don't know for sure what that means.

My mom used her purple pen. She filled up the rest of the space with writing to me. I like purple. It is hard work, but I read all the words she wrote. They say

Keith, you're real grown up now. I got to take this chance to make a life for myself. Jerry wants it to be just him and me. Jerry says you'll be okay, and you'd be leaving home real soon anyway. Jerry heard him and me could live real cheap in Mexico, so we're heading there. I'll try to write you when I get an address.

The rent's paid until the end of the month, and here's all the cash I got. Buy yourself something special for your birthday to remember your old mom. You be strong, son. Don't you be getting mad at me for going. I did my best. Life ain't easy for anyone.

She ran out of room for the "Love, Mom" part. But I don't know how I could find her to tell her.

JOE

At dinner, I think about telling my mom and dad about the way I'm going to help with this guy's proposal tonight; because my mom really likes romantic stuff and because it's just so amazing what's happened to my life in the past two days. But then I think again. My parents might say, "Just who is this man you're thinking of helping? How do you know him?" And I don't exactly think they'd approve of hearing that I met him as I was standing on a street corner panhandling.

Besides, I don't want Dad to give me a lecture about how if the girl is really worth it, she'd be perfectly happy to see me in the family's old minivan. And I certainly don't want Mom saying she'd like to come to Burger

84

Heaven, pretend she's a customer, and watch the whole engagement take place. So I don't say anything at dinner. After dinner, I mention I'm heading to Aaron's house, because that will never create any questions. He's the only person in school more boring than me, which may be why we're friends. Besides, I'm not exactly lying. Maybe I really will go over to Aaron's later.

Burger Heaven is only about a mile from my house. I walk toward the intersection where I'm supposed to meet Derrick, whose last name I don't know. What's that matter? I tell myself. It's his car I want, not his name. But as I'm walking, I start getting this sort of weird feeling. I mean, if I don't even know this guy, why would he let me borrow his truck, especially when that truck looks brand new? And what kind of a way is this to ask a girl to get married? And how stupid am I going to feel running into the restaurant holding a toy gun? What if there's someone I know in there? What if this whole thing is some kind of reality-TV prank like on *Punk'd*, and I'm the joke? How do I go back to school and live that down?

I stop at a light about a block from where I'm supposed to meet Derrick. It turns green, but I still stand right where I am because I'm starting to think that maybe . . . maybe this whole thing isn't such a good idea.

DYLAN

I am taking my final surveillance of the area before I meet the kid who's going to be my accomplice. This Joe will do just fine for tonight. It was almost too easy to find him. But Machiavelli said, "He who will trick will always find another who will suffer to be tricked." Certainly, I am a master trickster, and as for Joe, well, he was certainly easy to deceive. If he decides he didn't really want to rob the place once we've done it, I'll be happy to assist him by taking all the money for myself.

I must remember I told Joe my name is Derrick. No point in giving him any information he doesn't need. Ah . . . and there he is, right on time. I see him, a figure in the distance, heading this way, and I wait. He gets a block away from our meeting point, but he doesn't come any closer.

Then suddenly he turns and heads back the way he came.

My first thought is: "Damn Greg! Why'd he have to get arrested when I had a job for him! How irresponsible was that!" But there's no time for self-pity. This job takes two people to do it without getting caught. Joe is the only prospect I've got for tonight, so he's going to have to skip the cold feet. I gun the motor and pull up alongside of him, thinking fast.

"Hey, I saw you walking." I don't mention that it was in the wrong direction. Instead, I say, "I got here a little early because I thought you might like to try her out." Then I open the driver's door and wait. Watching him struggle with himself, I wonder, has this kid ever lived at all? Before he can say no, I get him behind the wheel. The look on his face is like a little kid's at Christmas. While he drives, I tell him all he wants to hear about my soon-to-be "fiancée." It's a good story, even for me.

He tells me he has to confess that he's only gotten to drive his parents' minivan.

"Well, this is not your parents' minivan. Go ahead, give it some gas," I encourage him.

"It's got great power." The look on his face is pure joy.

"Oh, yeah," I say, "it's a power ride, but wait until you have that girl sitting right next to you tomorrow, and then see how it feels!"

When we pull up in front of Burger Heaven, we are right on schedule, and he truly believes the two of us are good buddies. We're just a couple of guys helping each other out with our women.

Yeah. I really am that good.

KEITH

I want my mom to still be here. Maybe I made her mad. But I don't know what I did. Maybe it is just that I am me. Sometimes, that makes Mom mad. Sometimes, she tells me I got to be smart instead of dumb. I try to be smart. I try every day.

I watch at the park. Other moms push their kids on the swings. Then those moms and those kids go home. Everyone leaves the park. I see lights go on in the apartments. I think they are eating their dinners. I am still in the park. I am all by myself. I am sad.

Miss Simcor said people do special things for birthdays. I was going to ask my mom if we could go to Burger Heaven. It's my birthday. It's my favorite place.

Especially because sometimes, there's this really nice girl there named Jordan, and she says hi to me. She says she doesn't like ketchup on her burgers, either.

But Mom isn't here. Nobody is here. Maybe I could go to Burger Heaven anyway. I have the money in my hand. It was in my card. Maybe Jordan would be there. If I said it was my birthday, maybe Jordan would sing the song to me. Maybe Jordan would even want to sit down and talk to me. It's light in Burger Heaven. Maybe I wouldn't feel so scared there.

CONFRONTATION

ROBBERY IN PROGRESS

JOE: For the tenth time, Derrick has me go over the plan. I tell him that I've got it. I'll do everything right. I tell him he doesn't have to worry; I'm actually a pretty smart guy.

DYLAN/DERRICK: The problem with Joe is that he thinks he can think. All I need tonight is an extra pair of hands to hold a gun. The only brain invited or required will be mine.

JOE: Derrick reminds me that if I follow directions tonight, tomorrow I'll be driving my girl in his F-150. But I'm not even thinking about his truck right now because he's just handed me a gun! I feel like fireworks are popping in my insides. I almost laugh out loud. Me. Mr. Bland. I mean . . . I'm holding a gun . . . a real gun. I thought it was going to be a toy. It's so heavy. It feels cold in my hand. Okay, so it's not loaded, but still . . .

9:30 P.M., BURGER HEAVEN: THE BACK BOOTH BEHIND THE CHILDREN'S PLAYGROUND

MANUEL: Mrs. Wilkins knows all about this thing called a FAFSA application. She says these can actually get people money. Mrs. Wilkins says she'll help me with mine. She makes it all sound so possible . . . me . . . college. It's weird how life is. One day I'm working the drive-though at Burger Heaven; the next I'm thinking I can go to college.

SARA: This is so not fair! I mean, hello! I'm not the maid here. The schedule says three of us are on front-end tonight. Okay, so maybe Jordan does have to check out, but Manuel . . . he needs to fill the condiment and napkin holders so, like, maybe those of us who have a life can get to it.

MANUEL: I owe Jordan big-time. She doesn't tell Sara I'm sitting in the one booth Sara can't see from the front. I do feel a little bad. I should be helping with the shutdown, but Mrs. Wilkins is talking about how I'll have to get some information from my mom for the FAFSA scholarship. I don't want to miss any of this. I've got to make sure I understand it so I can translate it for my mom.

9:40 P.M., BURGER HEAVEN PARKING LOT

JOE: I put the gun back down on my lap long enough to pull on a black ski mask. I take a quick look in the rearview mirror to see what I look like as a "bandit." Pretty scary . . . only my eyes and the slit of my mouth show through the blackness.

DYLAN/DERRICK: I've been watching—no new cars in or out of the lot. The only ones left must be from employees. Good thing they keep these places so well lighted. It's easy to look in from the car and see that the place is deserted. Don't want to take a chance on them locking up early tonight. I need the doors to be open. "All right, it's time," I tell Joe.

JOE: Opening the car door, I take a deep breath and pick up the gun in my right hand. The door closes softly behind me, and I walk in the quiet darkness to the Burger Heaven entrance. For just an instant, I fumble with the door handle. For just an instant, I almost turn around and go back to the car. I can't pretend to be a robber. They'll all laugh at me.

DYLAN/DERRICK: What's the delay? I've manipulated this pawn so that he should do exactly what I've instructed. I've made him feel excitement, power, and promised reward. So why doesn't he open that door? *Now!* I shout silently.

JOE: Looking at the gun, I think I'll never have another experience like this one. I'm always too scared, too safe, to have any real fun. Why can't I do this? I'll just pretend I'm someone like Derrick. That'll work. I yank open the door just the way he would. Then I'm inside under the bright lights.

9:45 P.M., ONE AND A HALF MILES FROM BURGER HEAVEN

KEITH: When I get to Burger Heaven, I want a big, big fries. I might get two orders. I will blow on them if they are too hot. I know that. I won't burn my mouth. It's my birthday.

9:45 P.M., BURGER HEAVEN, IN THE BACK

ALEX: Kitchen's closing down—no reason not to clean off the grill now. We still have some burgers that are warm—good enough for any late-date losers that come in the next ten minutes. Jordan doesn't ever need to know.

9:45 P.M., BURGER HEAVEN, AT THE FRONT COUNTER

JORDAN: I hear the door open. The last thing I want to see is another customer, but it isn't ten o'clock yet, and I'm supposed to be the one in charge. I guess that means I shouldn't set a bad example by shouting out that we're closed before it's time. I keep counting my drawer as I automatically start to say, "Welcome to Burger Heaven. . . ."

JOE: The register girl looks at me, sees the ski mask and the gun. Her mouth makes this little O, and she gasps. She seems one hundred percent surprised and one hundred percent scared. She's good, maybe she's in drama at school. And then I think Derrick probably had her rehearse her scared look in front of a mirror. He seems to think of everything.

9:45 P.M., BURGER HEAVEN, IN THE BACK

THERESA: God, I wouldn't want to eat off any grill Alex ever cleaned. It's enough to make me give up fast food, not that I'd eat it anyway.

JOE: I hear a voice in the back; got to let 'em know I'm here. I shout, "Listen up. I've got a gun. Nobody gets hurt if everybody moves over by the grill." I sound like some cheesy movie, but I wave the gun toward them like I mean it, and they all move by the grill. This is actually pretty fun. I make my voice sound tougher. "Now! You get down, now, and you won't get hurt. Do it. Now! Drop to the floor facedown, hands over your head. Move!" And I think, do I sound like a great bad guy or what?

ALEX: I don't think that could be Jason—mask makes it hard to know for sure. I mean, yeah, I hit on his sister, and yeah, he said he'd kill me. But we were just being guys. At least, that's what I thought.

Better get down on the ground. No point in taking any chances.

Meanwhile, maybe he better watch out himself. Probably only another minute before Theresa gets ticked off enough to clobber him with ketchup or beat him on the head with frozen burgers.

JOE: They're all lying on the ground, and I'm standing over them like I'm this giant with a gun. God, but there is this amazing sense of power. It surges like lightning shooting through my body. I know this is all just pretend, and I know it's about to end, but I swear, even without the truck, I will never forget this night. I just wish I had a camcorder so I could prove I really did it. And I wish Derrick didn't have to come in yet to play the hero for Maria. My part went way too fast.

SARA: So, like, maybe I should be scared, but I think I'm just p.o.'d I'm lying here on this disgusting floor. Oh, my god, this glob of dried ketchup by my face is too gross. This guy with the gun—he's probably short on cash, but aren't we all? I'm trying not to gag on the stink of the spilled French fry grease. Let him get his money and get out.

DYLAN/DERRICK: I watch the seconds tick away on my Rolex. Joe has two more minutes to get the staff lying on the floor. If anything goes amiss and for some absurd reason the universe is misaligned, I won't enter Burger Heaven at all. My new "partner" doesn't know my last name or even my real first name, so I'll just let him be arrested for an inane story—that no cop anywhere would believe—while I fade away.

JORDAN: Lying here, I feel the keys in my pocket digging into my hip bone. I move a little to shift my weight, and the guy with the gun shouts, "Just stay right where you are!" I freeze, trying not to wince as the jagged edge of the key cuts into my hip.

I feel guilty, as if somehow this were my fault. I am the one in charge. Would Maria have done something differently to keep the employees safe?

JOE: There's this one guy who's about twice my size, but he says for me to stay cool with the gun because "nobody's moving." I don't care if this is all a game. It's so amazing. I tell him, "You got that right!" That's not in Derrick's script, but that's okay. Hey, might as well enjoy the last few seconds of my role.

DYLAN/DERRICK: Time for me to make my entrance for another successful evening. Pulling on the ski mask, I am again annoyed by its scratchiness and glad that tonight will be the last of this. I close the door to the truck. It's a pretty nice one, better than some of the others I've taken. Too bad I'll have to return it to its garage before its owner gets back into town and discovers it missing. Ah well . . . pretty soon, I'll have more than enough capital to buy whatever I want.

9:50 P.M., INSIDE BURGER HEAVEN

JOE: I glance over to see the door open. I'm hoping maybe Derrick has a camera in his pocket so he can get a picture of Maria saying yes, and if he does, maybe he could snap a quick picture of me like this, just so I could show everyone I really did it.

DYLAN/DERRICK: I like what I see. Joe has been a good little puppet. The store is quietly empty, and the employees are all lying on the floor just the way they should.

ALEX: Uh-oh—another one. So it can't be Jason. Didn't really think so, but . . .

DYLAN/DERRICK: "Maria," I say, "I want you to stand up now." That idiot Joe actually gives me a thumbs-up sign as if he still expects that I'm going to propose to this Maria. He's even more annoying than this stupid ski mask. However, I know that in five minutes, I'll be rid of both Joe and the mask.

I don't know which one Maria is, but I do know Maria is the manager on duty today because I checked earlier. Easy enough to find her. "Maria," I say to the prone bodies, "Get up, *now!*"

JOE: No one stands up. Maybe Maria isn't going to like this whole bad guy/good guy proposal idea. I probably should have mentioned that, but what do I know about girls? Poor Derrick. He's gone to so much trouble, and he loves her so much. If only Maria could have heard all the wonderful things he told me about her when we were in the truck. The truck! Oh no! I can feel my heart start to pound. Stand up, Maria! What if she doesn't? What if Derrick gets mad and storms off? What if I never get to borrow that truck? That can't happen!

Maria, *please*, just stand up and say yes! Then everyone can be happy.

9:52 P.M., NINE BLOCKS FROM BURGER HEAVEN

KEITH: It seems so long to walk to Burger Heaven. I wish I was already there. I might work at Burger Heaven someday. Then I could have lots of French fries.

9:52 P.M., BURGER HEAVEN, IN THE BACK

DYLAN/DERRICK: I look at the prone bodies on the floor. I will not risk being caught because of their game playing; I'm in somewhat of a hurry. I place the gun barrel next to a girl's head who might or might not be Maria. "What's your name?" I ask.

Her choked response: "Theresa."

"Okay, boys and girls," I say, "I have a gun at Theresa's head. So, Maria, why don't you stand up now and help Theresa out."

9:56 P.M., SIX BLOCKS FROM BURGER HEAVEN

KEITH: Last year, Mom took me to a movie for my birthday. This year is my Burger Heaven birthday.

9:56 P.M., BURGER HEAVEN, IN THE BACK

THERESA: I can't see the man because my head is turned the other way, but I can feel the gun he is pressing into the back of my neck. "Maria is not here," I say. The gun presses harder into my neck, and the voice asks, if Maria isn't here, am I the one in charge? I, who pride myself on being strong and standing up to crap, I, who work out every day and have sworn to always fight back, I force my body not to flinch at his gun. He will not shoot. He is a bully like so many others. I will not give him the satisfaction of a response.

101

SARA: Like, oh my gawd . . . This is so way out of hand. Why doesn't Theresa talk? I'd tell him if he had the gun on me. I, like, start to open my mouth, but then I think, What if he puts the gun on me? *I could die!* So for once, I button it up.

THERESA: The round steel presses into my neck. I try to block the memories of my stepdad standing over my mom. The guy says he is going to count to three, and then he'll pull the trigger and go to the next person. I always said I'd stand up to a bully, but here I am . . . so strong until it counts . . . all I can think is that I don't want to die. I silently apologize to Jordan. Then a voice—my voice—says Jordan is the one in charge. The scared me who fooled herself into believing she was strong volunteers that Maria's baby got sick, and Maria had to go home, and that's why Jordan is in charge. Maybe until now, I never really understood Mama's fear.

DYLAN/DERRICK: Joe begins talking. I tell him to shut up. He looks at me like some wounded puppy. And I tell Jordan to stand up now, or I'm going to shoot Theresa.

9:59 P.M., BURGER HEAVEN

JOE: Suddenly, nothing makes sense. I tell Derrick that I've had enough. I'm leaving. This isn't funny, and it isn't right. He doesn't say anything, doesn't move the gun from the girl. So I tell him to keep his gun and his truck .

. . I am out of here right now. All the power, all the strength, all the fun I was having . . . gone.

THERESA: Good, good, good, my heart pounds, hoping that they will leave. I try not to look at the mask of white that is Jordan's face. "I'm so sorry," I mouth, but it doesn't help. How could it? I know too much of helpless apologies.

DYLAN/DERRICK: Annoying. Joe hasn't been dismissed. He is still needed here, and thus, he will remain and follow my directions. I'll deal with him in a minute. First, I need to get the manager in action.

JOE: "I'm not staying here. I mean it, Derrick," I say. I start to walk away, but then I notice one of the girls lying on the floor is shaking. I'm responsible for her being that afraid, and I can't leave until I make things right. Derrick is sick. He does all this for power over people; first me, now them.

JORDAN: I don't move. I don't want to leave whatever safety there is in being with the rest of them. I have this irrational urge to explain that I can't die here. This is only a forgettable high school job. I'm supposed to go to college, to live a life. My family, my friends, everyone expects me to be someone.

JOE: It was all part of his power trip to make me follow every one of his stupid instructions, and I, like a fool, did it. But I know this isn't a real robbery. Derrick doesn't need the money. Look at the truck he drives. He's just playing games . . . like the jocks who trashcan kids because it's fun. "Hey," I say, "relax, these guns aren't even loaded. Derrick here was supposed—"

DYLAN/DERRICK: "These guns are very loaded, and you don't want to find that out by having one of them shot at you. So you'll stay right where you are." I glance at Joe with disgust.

"And you . . . before you think about leaving, you better try letting your small brain really think, for once in your life."

10:01 P.M., THREE BLOCK FROM BURGER HEAVEN

KEITH: Fifty-one, fifty-two, fifty-three, fifty-four . . . I'm getting closer to Burger Heaven!

10:01 P.M., IN BURGER HEAVEN

DYLAN/DERRICK: "Joe, you are the one who perpetrated this robbery. You are the one who walked in here with a gun. Four witnesses will testify to the fact that they're on the floor now because you waved a gun at them. If we get caught, you're going to jail."

JOE: Jail? Robbery? I look down at the hand that is holding a loaded gun. What have I done?

10:02 P.M., BURGER HEAVEN, IN THE FRONT

MANUEL: I whisper to Mrs. Wilkins, "I can't tell for sure what they're saying, but I think they're talking to each other." At least me and Mrs. Wilkins are both under this table, and I'm pretty sure the guy has no idea that we're here. I tell Mrs. Wilkins that maybe I could sneak out and get help, but she puts her hand on my arm and whispers back that I should wait until we can decide exactly where the robbers are in the store. "We've just got your future figured out," she said. "We're not going to end it before it's even started."

MRS. WILKINS: I'm trying so hard to be brave for Manuel. I don't want him doing anything foolish, but I feel like ten thousand needles are piercing the hip I broke last year. The pain from my arthritis is worse . . . I need desperately to stand up. I almost think I'd risk getting shot just to stand up, but I can't risk Manuel's life. I'm fairly certain we're safe, as long as we both stay down here.

10:04 P.M., BURGER HEAVEN, IN THE BACK

JORDAN: The guy in charge calls my name, and it sounds like a terrible curse. The key in my pocket has dug a hole in my hip, but I don't move even a muscle. The guy walks over to Sara, kicks her, and says, "Get up!" Sara sobs, "Not me . . . Jordan's the redhead." The next thing I know, a hand is roughly pulling me up and shoving me to the front counter. The in-charge guy throws a back-pack at me, tells me to go open the underneath part of each cash register, and pull out the big bills. Then he says we'll go in the back and unlock the safe, and he'll be out of here. No one will get hurt. I feel I am two people, and I am watching myself in this crazy nightmare that cannot be real.

SARA: When the backpack Bossy One goes up in front, maybe I can convince this one to let me go. He is shaking, and I think maybe he's going to put down his gun. They don't need all of us. . . . Maybe I'll flash him some thigh, and for a little look-see, he can, like, let me out of here.

ALEX: I'm thinking about going after this robber's gun. He looks scared and he's not that big. Girls love guys who've faced danger head-on. I'm ready.

But then the lead robber, on his way to the front, stops and whispers something to this one. I don't know what, but the guy back here, his whole attitude changes, and it leaves me thinking I better not move.

JOE: Derrick whispers that if I don't make any mistakes here, we'll both get out; no one will be hurt, and I can live the rest of my life like tonight never happened. I try to protest, but his voice gets real soft, and he describes what my first night in jail would be like. I can't live through that. The only way out is . . .

10:05 P.M., OUTSIDE BURGER HEAVEN

KEITH: One hundred and ninety, one hundred and ninety-one, one hundred and ninety-two, one hundred and ninety-three . . . I'm here! I'm at Burger Heaven. The people here are nice. I see Jordan through the window. I like Jordan. I will tell her it is my birthday. Jordan will be happy. I open the door.

10:05 P.M., INSIDE BURGER HEAVEN, AT THE COUNTER

JORDAN: I am trembling so hard, I can't fit the key in the register lock. I have to hold my wrist with my other hand to steady it. "Hurry, hurry!" the guy in charge keeps commanding me. He's crouched down. I look like I'm standing here all alone, but his eyes watch me put every bit of money into his backpack.

KEITH: "Hi Jordan! It's me." I am happier than all night.

JORDAN: The gun guy frowns as Keith walks in the door. Poor, sweet Keith. What has he stumbled into? I think I could be his death or he could be our salvation. Oh, Keith, I ask, can you comprehend enough to know how much is wrong?

DYLAN/DERRICK: Another complication. I'm definitely going to earn my money tonight. I thought about locking the doors when I came in, but they're a double-key lock, and I didn't want to take the time to fool with them. I guess this kid can join the others on the floor.

JORDAN: If only Keith can get out of here. . . . What can I say to make him understand?

KEITH: "Hi, Jordan. Guess what? It's my birthday."

JORDAN: I know I can't let him get all the way to the counter because then he'll see the robber, and then the robber will make Keith go with the others. All those critical thinking exercises . . . and when I need it most I cannot seem to think at all. "Uhh . . . We're closed!" I bark. "Go somewhere else."

KEITH: Jordan is never mean, never. But she's being mean now. I tell Jordan, "I'm eighteen today, but my mom left, and—" I try to explain to Jordan. She won't listen. She even interrupts. I say, "Miss Simcor says we shouldn't interrupt people when they're—" Jordan still doesn't listen. Jordan says, "Go tell someone else your problems, not me. We're closed. Get out!" She yells at me.

SARA: Oh—*gawd!* The guy with the gun on us jumps a little when Jordan screams. It's like living a nightmare. I've pulled up my stupid Burger Heaven skirt enough to give this gun guy a lot of eye candy, and, like, lots of guys have been plenty impressed, but this one—nothing.

KEITH: I don't want to cry in front of Jordan, so I walk out the door. The clock says 10:05. It's only five minutes late. It's my birthday. People think I don't know anything. I do. I can tell time. I'm mad. I start to walk away. But it's not fair. Everyone is mean to me. I am never mean to them. It's light and bright inside Burger Heaven. I want to be there. My fists just start to pound on the window. "It's not fair. It's not fair!" I shout. My fists pound harder on the window. "It's my birthday!" I shout.

OFFICER RICK JEFFRIES: Pulling a double shift is tough. And tonight's already been way too busy. A hit-and-run, a burglary, a domestic violence call, and my second shift has hours to go. Everyone wants law and order, but no one wants to be a cop, so we're always shorthanded. God, I'm so tired. I think I'll stop by Burger Heaven. It's close, and if they're still open, I could grab an extra-large coffee, a megadose of caffeine. Besides, if Alex still works there, I can remind him again about going back to school. I don't know why I can't get through to that kid. The others I've mentored have at least been willing to listen.

DYLAN/DERRICK: Damn . . . that moron outside is pounding on the window. He's like a neon sign that shouts trouble. "Joe! Get out there and get that kid. Bring him in here," I order. But Joe doesn't move. Greg would have known how to take care of this, but Greg had to get himself in a fight and in jail. The problem with this world is that a reasonable person such as myself can't rely on anyone.

10:08 P.M., BURGER HEAVEN

OFFICER JEFFRIES: Just as I start to pull into the Burger Heaven lot, I see a male, about five feet eleven, take a rock and throw it through the window of the store. I call it in and get out of the car. I don't see a weapon, but I take no chances. "Police!" I yell. "Put your hands in the air." He does. "Now, lie on the ground, keep your hands and feet where I can see them."

KEITH: "I didn't do nothing. I didn't do nothing." I try to tell the policeman about what happened. He doesn't listen. He pulls my arms behind me. It hurts. He puts on handcuffs. I cry. "Who's in there?" the policeman just shouts at me. He won't listen. That makes me cry harder.

The policeman puts me in the back of his car. He shuts the door. He walks into Burger Heaven. My face feels all wet. I don't know if it's crying or blood or both.

10:18 P.M., BURGER HEAVEN

JORDAN: The door to Burger Heaven opens, and my first thought is "Thank God!" as I see a big police officer walk through it. "Are you okay, miss?" he asks. "Is everything here okay?"

I feel like screaming at him that everything is *not* okay. A guy with a gun is sitting down behind the counter, and that gun is pressed into my spine. The rest of the crew is in the back on the floor, and another guy back there is holding a gun on them. He's so jittery that he might accidentally shoot them. But I don't reveal any of those things. The gun presses into my back a little harder. I only take a small breath and say, "It's fine, Officer."

DYLAN/DERRICK: Her response is insufficient. She should be upset that someone threw a rock through the window. She's got to let the officer know that she's upset so he'll decide that everything is normal and go away. I'm starting to get one of my migraine headaches. Why can't any of these people think! I certainly can't say anything to Jordan right now. The muzzle of the gun will have to speak for me.

OFFICER JEFFRIES: I ask the young woman her name. Then I ask again if everything is okay, and if she knows the boy who threw the rock through the glass. She tells me his name is Keith, and he's a little slow, if I understand. He's a longtime regular customer. She says they were getting ready to close, and Keith got angry.

JOE: Part of me wants to put down this gun and run out to the police officer. I was a Boy Scout. I don't rob places. But I did come into this one with a gun, which I waved around, and I did order everyone down on the ground. How could I have been so stupid! Even if I could get to that cop, would he ever believe my story? Derrick's jail scene plays out in my brain. I stay frozen in the kitchen area.

OFFICER JEFFRIES: I don't get out my pad and pen to take down Jordan's comments. I sense something very wrong. I don't see any other workers. One girl wouldn't be here alone. Has this kid in my car hurt the others? "Well," I say, stalling for time, "I guess I'll go deal with this Keith." I walk toward the counter. "Tell you what. Here's my card. If you have anything further to add, you'll call me." I put the card on the counter. Years of police work have taught me to maintain absolutely no change in expression as my eye catches a glimpse of a gun muzzle in the girl's back.

10:24 P.M., BURGER HEAVEN

DYLAN/DERRICK: That cop shouldn't have left so fast. He didn't even get Jordan's full name or ask for any other witnesses to the rock throwing. Why not? He must suspect something else going on. Question is, does he have a partner staked out at the back door, or can I take this backpack and get out before backup arrives. It isn't enough cash, but sometimes, you've got to cut your losses. I don't need the extra baggage of Joe or anyone knowing which way I went. The truck will have to stay. That's okay. It wasn't really mine anyway. Time is of the essence. Got to move. Got to go. *Now.*

JORDAN: He pulls my arm behind my back and makes me walk in front of him. He is taller, which makes my arm pull up high and hurts bad. "Where are we going?" I can hear the fear in my voice. But he doesn't say anything, just pushes me in front of him. I stumble backward, and as I catch myself, my head bangs into his chest. He laughs and tells me he's not interested. I shudder.

10:28 P.M., BURGER HEAVEN

THERESA: I see Jordan's and the robber's legs walk by us in the kitchen. She's begging him to not hurt her, but he doesn't say anything. I ask the Virgin Mary to keep her safe, but it's not enough. I was the one who told who she was. I have to do something. Otherwise, I am no better than those who stand by. So what if I work on the Teen Crisis Line, if I am too frightened to help in my own crisis.

I turn my head toward the ski-masked guy that the other one called Joe. He's still pointing a gun at us. "You don't have to do this," I say. "Help us, and we'll all tell the police that he made you do this. We'll be on your side."

ALEX: I tell Theresa to shut up. I don't really care if he shoots her . . . but I am lying close enough that I might get hit too.

DYLAN/DERRICK: I move the girl to the back door. I'll open it. If there's a cop there, she's my shield, and we'll both step back inside. If there are no cops, I'll knock her out and take off. I'm not panicked because I don't exhibit that emotion. Panic is for fools, and it forces them to make foolish mistakes. I am not a fool.

MANUEL: It's so quiet now. I don't have any idea what's happening or where anyone is. I think maybe I should try to crawl out from under the table and sneak out for help. I try to move. I'm wedged in so tightly, and Mrs. Wilkins groans as I try to get around her. I freeze. Did they hear the sound?

10:31 P.M., BURGER HEAVEN

OFFICER MARC BAUMEL: I hear the radio call about a possible robbery at the Burger Heaven at Tatum and Cactus. I'm almost there, so I radio that I'll take backup. If it turns out to be nothing, at least I'll get a cup of coffee. I pull up at the back of the place, but before I can get around front to talk to the other cop, I see the door open, and there's movement.

My spotlight beam illuminates a frightened-looking girl standing in front of a tall man. I start to shout *freeze*, but the couple retreats back into the restaurant, and the door slams shut.

10:33 P.M., BURGER HEAVEN

JOE: Derrick shoves the girl onto the floor. He stands over everyone, gun pointed. His voice sounds so calm as he tells me that we're going to have to keep these masks on for a little while longer. "Is somebody out there?" I ask. Derrick doesn't answer, except to say that everything will work out.

SARA: "Jordan," I whisper, "any way out of here?" But the guy in charge grabs my ponytail and yanks my head up.

"Shhh," he says. "No one asked you to speak, okay?" I am, like, so beyond petrified.

JOE: "Please . . . Derrick . . . you don't need me to stay here anymore. This was all a huge mistake. I don't want to hurt anyone. I don't want any money. I don't want your truck. I just want tonight never to have happened. You go ahead and get all the money. *Please*—just let me leave."

Then Derrick tells me I can go. I can really go. But first, I have to tape everyone up. There's a big roll of silver duct tape on the counter. Derrick tells me to wrap it around each person's feet four or five times. "Make it tight," he says. He picks up a napkin, takes my gun from my hand, and stands pointing both guns at us. And I know I started all this, but I swear, I'm as scared of Derrick as they are.

THERESA: "I'm so sorry," the guy tells me as he winds the sticky tape around my ankles. I can feel my bones press into each other. He apologizes to every one of us as he binds us, but he doesn't stand up to Derrick, doesn't try to stop him. After our feet are all bound, he follows Derrick's instructions to pull our hands behind our backs and duct-tape them together. When he tapes Alex, the silver goes right over the snake tattoo Alex is so proud of. As the tape wraps its way around my arms, I bite my lip from the pain of my old broken wrist—a reminder of my stepfather's drunken rages.

DYLAN/DERRICK: Now that the hostages are bound, I can manage without Joe. Still, he might create an interesting diversion for the police, if necessary, at some point. It would probably help to have him stick around now, if only to create confusion later. So I tell him how the police will find his fingerprints on the gun. I tell him how he willingly entered and did this, and changing his mind later doesn't alter the initial facts. I describe jail to him again. This time, I go into more detail about what will happen to a fresh young thing like him.

ALEX: Man, it's awful, but that stuff he's saying . . . I think it's true. And not just from TV. I had a cousin, a little guy, and what got done to him in jail . . .

DYLAN/DERRICK: I walk over to Joe, slowly and deliberately. I put the gun back in his hand, and he takes it. Good. He cannot make eye contact with me, and it is evident that they all get the message: I and only I am in charge here. Joe will do exactly what I want him to do, and so will they.

11:00 P.M., OUTSIDE BURGER HEAVEN, NEXT TO YELLOW POLICE TAPE

JILLIAN KWAN: This is Jillian Kwan, with a late-breaking bulletin from KNKV, Channel 16, with Valley news you can count on. At this moment, police are clearing an area in the vicinity of Cactus and Tatum, where they suspect a robbery gone bad may have turned into a hostage situation. We have been unable to learn the exact number of robbers or hostages. The police are using bullhorns, trying to make contact with the robber or robbers.

We'll update you just as soon as we know more. Meanwhile, stay tuned to KNKV, with Valley news you can count on.

11:00 P.M., INSIDE BURGER HEAVEN

DYLAN/DERRICK: The phone in Burger Heaven begins ringing insistently. I quit counting after ten and pour myself some cold coffee. I need quiet time to think, but police bullhorns blast, "Pick up the phone; let us know what you want."

What I want is for them to go away; what I want is to take the cash I came here to get; what I want is to get on with my life and forget this botched disaster. Unfortunately, I feel certain that what the police want and what I want are not even remotely close.

11:03 P.M., BURGER HEAVEN

JOE: Derrick orders me to turn off the lights. Tells me there's no point in giving the police a lighted portrait of us all. I say okay. Even though I look down and see the gun in my hand, I cannot believe this is actually happening.

I want to wake up from this awful dream. But the nightmare is real. I started this mess. I have to be the one to stop it. I reach for the lights. I just hope I don't throw up or pass out. My pastor would be so ashamed that I am praying to hurt someone with a gun, but I don't think Derrick will let any of these people leave. I have to stop Derrick.

All at the same time, I flip the lights, fire the gun, and scream, "I'm so sorry, Derrick!"

The gun practically jumps from my hand, and I realize that my eyes are squeezed shut.

In the darkness, there is a wailing scream, but it is too high pitched to be Derrick. Oh, god. What have I done?

11:05 P.M., OUTSIDE BURGER HEAVEN

JILLIAN KWAN: This is Jillian Kwan, with a late-breaking bulletin from KNKV, Channel 16, with Valley news you can count on. Behind me you can see the yellow tape cordoning off the area around Burger Heaven. We have just heard what we believe is the sound of a gunshot from the restaurant, but at this time, we are unable to confirm the source of that sound. People are being asked to stay away from the area.

We'll update you with more news as soon as it breaks. Meanwhile, stay tuned to Channel 16, with Valley news you can count on.

11:05 P.M., INSIDE BURGER HEAVEN

JOE: A girl's voice keeps screaming, "Oh—no—no—I've been shot! I've been shot! Help me!" I turn on the light in the kitchen. The girl is still screaming, and I feel frozen to the spot where I am standing as I see red blood coming from her shoulder.

My life has ended. I have just killed someone.

11:10 P.M., NORTHEAST PHOENIX POLICE STATION

KEITH: They got me milk at the police station. They said I could go home if I told them everything. I told them I didn't want to go home. I told them about how it was dark at home. They wanted to know about Burger Heaven. They said I could have a cookie if I told them everything I knew. I said, "Okay! When you bring me my cookie, could you sing 'Happy Birthday'?"

11:10 P.M., INSIDE BURGER HEAVEN

DYLAN/DERRICK: Well, isn't tonight filled with unwelcome surprises? I'd never have bet that Joe would actually have had enough nerve to fire a gun. It seems to have fired away his manhood, too. He's lying on the floor in a fetal position, crying. I walk over, using a dishrag to take his gun. I duct-tape one of his legs to the metal post in the kitchen. That should keep him out of the way and still available if I need him.

11:20 P.M., BURGER HEAVEN

JILLIAN KWAN: This is Jillian Kwan, from KNKV, Channel

16. We're live, reporting on the latest developments in the Burger Heaven hostage situation. It has been almost two hours since we first broke this story. Police are still keeping us behind this yellow tape, but we have learned that the police have made contact with at least one of the hostage takers. Though police are releasing no details of that conversation at this time, we'll let you know more as it becomes available.

In a KNKV exclusive, I am speaking with Ms. Berenice Martinez, whose daughter may be one of the hostages. "Ms. Martinez, your daughter works at Burger Heaven, is that correct?"

"Yes, and she never came home after work. I'm so scared. She is a good girl. She would have come home if she could."

"Ms. Martinez, have you any words for your daughter?"

"Theresa, if you can hear me, be brave. I love you. And to those people who are holding her, please, please don't hurt my baby. Please just let her go."

This is Jillian Kwan, reporting live. We'll update you with more news as it breaks. Meanwhile, stay tuned to KNKV, Channel 16, with Valley news you can count on.

MANUEL: In the darkness, I keep thinking about trying to crawl out, but then my brain replays the sound of that gunshot. They are not afraid to use their weapons. I don't want to die.

I am worried for Mrs. Wilkins. In just the sliver of light we have, I can see her face is lined with the pain she feels. I've managed to stretch her out. They cannot see her over here, and maybe lying flat eases the pain.

MRS. WILKINS: This has gone on too long for a happy ending. I may be an old woman, but I am not a naive one. My poor daughter. She will blame herself for not making me move to the retirement home and for not taking away my driver's license. Maybe, in the darkness, I could reach my purse and write a note for her. I will tell her that I loved her, and she was not to blame.

11:30 P.M., BURGER HEAVEN

ALEX: I think I hear Sara moan. "You okay?" She moans again. I tell her to try not to die. What else can I do?

11:40 P.M., BURGER HEAVEN

DYLAN/DERRICK: The police negotiators keep asking me what I want. I tell them I'll let them know. It's important to keep control as I try to discern what the police would be willing to give me that would actually assist me. Meanwhile, I keep reassuring everyone—the police and these hostages—that I don't have any interest in hurting anyone. *If* everyone stays calm and follows my directives.

SARA: There's sticky blood on the floor next to me—my blood—I never knew blood had such an awful smell. I beg Derrick to let me go. I tell him that the police will want him to release a—hostage, yeah—a good-faith hostage. It's so not right for me to be here. Saturday night. I'm supposed to be at a party tonight, not on this floor with my hair in my own blood.

11:45 P.M., BURGER HEAVEN

MANUEL: Mrs. Wilkins and I have whispered our life stories to each other in the quiet darkness. It helps make the time pass and not be quite so terrible. I ask her to tell me again of the way she met her husband over sixty years ago, but there is no answer. "Mrs. Wilkins," I say softly. I nudge her. There is no response. I nudge her harder. "Please, please, say something!"

Finally, she gasps, "My heart . . . such pain . . . "

ALEX: Sara must be okay. Nobody dying could complain that much.

MANUEL: If I don't get Mrs. Wilkins out of here, she is going to die. I have to convince them to let her go. I try to make myself stand up, but I can't move. I tell myself I'm no better than they are. I'm more concerned about me than about someone else's life. I'm just so scared.

I take a deep breath. I've got to do this now. "Don't shoot!" I yell in a shaky voice. "I've been hiding under a table since the beginning. I don't have a weapon. There's an old lady with me. She had a heart attack. If you don't get her out of here, she's going to die." As I say this, I just hope she's not already dead. I hope they aren't going to kill me.

11:50 P.M., BURGER HEAVEN

DYLAN/DERRICK: What else could go wrong tonight! I tell the guy to lie down on the floor, right where he is, with his hands in front of him. I turn the flashlight I've found on low and move toward him. Behind him, in the ray of light, I can see the old woman. Quickly, I wrap duct tape around the boy's ankles and arms, just so there are no surprises from him.

MANUEL: He pushes at Mrs. Wilkins with the toe of his shoe, but Mrs. Wilkins doesn't open her eyes. He bends down and listens for her breathing. "Damn!" he whispers. Then he cuts the tape binding my hands and drags me over to Mrs. Wilkins. Asks me do I know CPR. I do—sort of. He tells me it's up to me if she lives or dies. I can't remember—how many breaths and how many compressions? My mind is blank. "Two and thirty," he says. "Now start!"

"Come on, Mrs. Wilkins! Breathe!"

11:55 P.M., BURGER HEAVEN

THERESA: While he's not standing over us, quick, can anyone move at all? If we could just get free . . . "Alex," I whisper urgently, "roll toward me, maybe I can loosen your tape with my feet."

ALEX: Oh, yeah, right, so now she wants me.

DYLAN/DERRICK: I detect a faint pulse starting. Nobody's dying on my watch. There's no statute of limitations when someone dies. I'm not looking over my shoulder for the rest of my life. I go to the phone, and I notice the one girl's foot wedged between a guy's feet trying to loosen the tape. I explode. "Can't anyone do what they're supposed to!"

THERESA: He grabs me by my hair and shoves me into the leg of the counter. He tapes me to the counter so I can't move. The steel leg cuts into my spine, but at least I tried to do something besides be a victim.

If only it had worked.

12:05 A.M., OUTSIDE BURGER HEAVEN

OFFICER JEFFRIES: Finally, it appears we've made a deal to get at least two hostages out. It's strange, though. The shooter still hasn't asked for anything. He just called us and said that we should have an ambulance waiting for an old woman who had a heart attack. He said a kid would be carrying her out.

We've got spotlights trained on the door and sharp-shooters ready to fire in case this is some sort of trick.

JILLIAN KWAN: This is Jillian Kwan, and you are seeing breaking news footage from our minicam of a teenage boy bringing one of the hostages out of the Burger Heaven restaurant. She's being placed into that ambulance.

We believe the boy may be another of the hostages, but police will know more as soon as they've finished questioning him. So far, no names have been released. We will stay with this story, reporting every detail as soon as it becomes available. Reporting live from KNKV, with Valley news you can count on.

12:10 A.M., INSIDE BURGER HEAVEN

SARA: Like, does no one care that I've cried so hard I'm hoarse? And now, he finally lets two hostages go, and I'm still here. "Derrick, please," I beg. "I *so* need help. I could die here." Derrick comes over to me. He bends down. Maybe he's going to let me go now, too. He looks at my shoulder, and then he just walks away.

DYLAN/DERRICK: I've checked this place, hoping for some exit I missed, but they're all clearly marked, and they're all covered by the police. There doesn't seem to be a way out of this for any of us. I announce that if anyone knows of any way out of here besides the doors, to speak up now before the police try a rescue. "You may think the police are on your side, but if they come in here shooting, some of you may get rescued, but some of you will undoubtedly be killed. And how can you know which you'll be?" I spell it out for them. The best way for all of them to live is to help me escape.

SARA: Oh, gawd, he's right. Last month, that movie with

that hot new actor—it was about a bank robbery. The police and the gunmen got in a fight, and everyone died. But what can we do? I feel like I'm in a brain meltdown. It's like there is no way out. Gawd, I could use a cigarette.

Wait . . . a cigarette. That's it—earlier this week—when I was out back for a smoke . . . I remember what I heard!

I call Derrick over. I tell him about how the day I went out for a smoke, I heard about Burger Heaven's new safe. But, like, he's not understanding. So I have to, like, slow down and explain that they cut a hole in the wall to put the safe in the back, but there was, like, a mix-up, and the safe didn't get delivered. That's when I, like, heard Tony—he's the owner's son—talking to his dad on a cell phone explaining how he, like, put this piece of plywood over the hole, like, where the safe was supposed to go, and shoved some file cabinets against it until the right safe comes. But the safe still hasn't come.

ALEX: Derrick starts listening real good to Sara. She promises it's all true.

12:20 A.M., BURGER HEAVEN

DYLAN/DERRICK: I place a piece of duct tape over each person's mouth so it's quiet. I may need time for an escape. Then in the back corner of the office, I push the file cabinets aside, and there is the plywood, and there is the hole, and just that simple—I'm out. No spotlights glaring. No one behind me. It's one of those things where real life is better than any movie.

It's only a few feet to some large oleander bushes, and I dive into them. The bushes stretch along the back of a block wall. Holding my breath, I jump up and leap over the wall. The darkness has done its job. No one has seen. I permit myself a small smile. When you're Dylan, life may not always be easy, but it always rights itself. Some other guy, he would have gotten caught tonight. I brush myself off, stand up, and walk down a street like anyone else. By the time the police storm the place, I will have been long gone. The backpack may not have as much cash as I need, but it's enough for a down payment. I can still meet my deadline, and the planets of the universe are realigned again.

12:45 A.M., OUTSIDE BURGER HEAVEN

JILLIAN KWAN: KNKV has followed the hostage story at Burger Heaven from the moment it started. And finally, we have breaking good news. The hostages have been freed. We repeat: The hostages have been freed. Police stormed the restaurant just minutes ago, after getting no answer to their calls. One of the robbers was apprehended, but one is still on the loose. We have been told that one hostage was found slightly injured and has gone to the hospital. The others are meeting with police. KNKV, Channel 16, with Valley news you can count on, will stay with this story for any further breaking news.

THERESA: Finally, they are finished with us. The police artist has been here and has tried to sketch the cruel eyes we have described. A policewoman thanks us all, tells us we have been a big help—but I don't think we have. Eyes without a face aren't much of a description. And then, at last, we are told that we can go home. My mother has held my hand for this whole time at the police station. Without words, we know how frightened we were of losing each other tonight. And I understand the helplessness that she must have felt with my stepdad in a way that I never could before.

JORDAN: I've never longed for anything more than just to crawl into my own bed, but I find myself reaching over to hug each of my fellow workers good-bye. They are not my friends; they probably never will be, and yet, I almost hate to leave them tonight.

NINE LIVES

ONE YEAR LATER

JORDAN

ASSIGNMENT: *In a paper of no less than 500 words and no more than 750 words, create a well-crafted essay that addresses a pivotal moment in your life.*

JORDAN M. ELLIS
UNIVERSITY OF ARIZONA
ID # 823001
ENGLISH 101
SECTION 15A
MIDTERM ASSIGNMENT

I felt the metal of a gun in my spine as the robber pulled me to the back door to be his possible shield. Though police had arrived outside the restaurant at which I worked, they seemed unable to help those of us inside who were hostages.

This was not part of a TV detective show or a big-screen adventure movie, but an actual moment from my life. However, although it was certainly a terrifying and dramatic one, it, in itself, was not the most pivotal. It may seem hard to believe, but that moment came later.

In the first shell-shocked week that followed the robbery, everyone was very considerate. They gave me space and time to recover. All my obligations were put on hold.

After seven tortured days, I still hadn't really made sense of it all, but my world felt I'd had enough time to recover. I needed to "buck up," to be the Jordan they expected. My AP teachers worried I'd get too far behind. My coach reminded me that he was counting on my help to conduct an important basketball clinic. My parents felt that I needed to keep working, but they wanted me to look for a safer job. And my counselor warned me that scholarship deadlines would pass with or without my personal traumas.

I thought I was managing well, until I started having severe stomach pains. "You might have food poisoning," my coach said. "It must be your appendix," my mother worried. "We've got to get her well quickly," my father reminded. "She has a college interview next week."

Finally, there was a visit to the emergency room, which revealed no food poisoning nor any appendicitis.

The doctor told us that my pain was simply the result of intense stress.

"Well, she has been through a robbery," my parents explained. But I knew it wasn't just that. And still, even with such knowledge assaulting my stomach nightly, it took me weeks before I could unpeel all the layers of pleasing everyone else enough to learn what might please me. And when I did so, that was the pivotal moment. How ironic that it took being held hostage before I was finally able to set myself free.

In learning to become myself, I was able, despite my counselor's confusion and my parents' puzzlement, to announce that I had decided not to try for one of *their* name universities. I realized I was doing it for them, instead of for me. That didn't mean I gave up learning or working; it was just that I no longer felt the responsibility to try to be perfect, to avoid disappointing anyone else.

After careful thought, my decisions led me here to U of A, where I am doing well and learning a lot. It's a great school, and it's plenty challenging academically. I've even declared a major for myself. I'm proud to have done so without checking with everyone else to see if it is permissible.

By majoring in psychology, I hope to better understand the *at-all-costs people-pleasing me* I used to be and learn how to avoid becoming that person ever again. Once I'm sure of who I am, I want to spend my career helping others who might be as lost to themselves as I once was.

ALEX

(On a street corner)

PAULIE:	That you, Alex? It is! Where've you been?
ALEX:	Gone.
PAULIE:	Well . . . duh, I figured that out. Gone where?
ALEX:	Hollywood.
PAULIE:	Hollywood? You kidding? Why?
ALEX:	Well . . . at Burger Heaven—I was lying on the floor—that crazy psycho waving his gun—I was thinking my whole career—my whole life—could be over. When I got out of there okay, I said *time to live right now!* Me and Socks took off the next day.

PAULIE:	You went to Hollywood, and you took the cat?
ALEX:	Socks isn't just a cat. He's *my* cat. At least girls like to pet him . . . you they run away from.
PAULIE:	Yeah, right, very funny. So, did you actually get to be in any movies?
ALEX:	Yeah.
PAULIE:	Really?
ALEX:	I just told you *yeah*.
PAULIE:	Then why're you back?
ALEX:	Socks . . . he missed it here.
PAULIE:	You crazy? You got in the movies, and you came back here because your dumb cat likes the garbage dump?
ALEX:	I told you the cat's not dumb. Hollywood's all screwed up. Guys that look good like me, they make them extras—treat them like crap. Faces never even show up on film. It's the freaks and the wimps that get the good parts and the food and the trailers and the women. Pretty soon nobody's going to even want to go to the movies.
PAULIE:	So how long you been back?
ALEX:	Couple weeks. Probably going to sign with an agent here.
PAULIE:	I didn't even know they made movies in Phoenix.
ALEX:	Maybe not as many as Hollywood, but I got a

better look for here. They don't want wimps here. Meantime, I'm back at Burger Heaven.

PAULIE: You gotta be kidding. I quit three months ago.

ALEX: Yeah, but I need a job where I can take off all the time when my agent calls—and he's probably going to be calling a lot. So Burger Heaven's just a temporary thing for me, till the big checks start rolling in. It's not all bad being back at BH—because working the counter is this really hot chick—maybe worth hooking up with until I leave—her name's Adrienne.

SARA

HEIDI: Thanks so much for talking with me, Sara. Can we just sit in this booth over here?

SARA: Uh, well, like, let's try over there instead. Marni washed that side. This is my side, and I, like, didn't feel like cleaning.

HEIDI: (*sitting where told*) As I explained on the phone, I want to do a feature story in the newspaper about crime victims and how the experience has affected their lives. Now, I'll turn on this little recorder and ask you a few questions. Okay?

SARA: Are you, like, going to take my picture, too, because this lip gloss, it doesn't stay on very long, so I'll, like, probably need to fix it, okay?

HEIDI: We may use pictures, but if so, I'll send a photographer another time.

SARA: Uhh, maybe I shouldn't tell you this, but I, like, don't really read the newspaper. Is this gonna be on TV, too?

HEIDI: Well, we do have a working arrangement with Channel 12, but right now, I think this is just going to be in the newspaper. Tell you what, let's get started. Now, last year, just about this time, you were shot in a robbery at this very restaurant. Can you tell me what happened after that—how you felt about things?

SARA: Okay. Yeah, I can do that. Well—I was, like, so gonna quit afterwards. I mean, I figure not even the court would make me work at a place where I could get killed, right? But then, my probation guy said I could, like, quit Burger Heaven, but I still had to work somewhere, and be responsible, and . . . blah, blah, blah, blah . . . you know. So, like, how am I doing? I've never been interviewed before.

HEIDI: You're doing great, just great. Now you were on probation for what?

SARA: Oh . . . I, like, so didn't mean to talk about that.

HEIDI: Well, the information might not even fit in the article, but why don't you tell me about it, since you've already started.

SARA: Well . . .

HEIDI: I'll bet you really didn't do anything that bad. Why not tell me what happened so I can understand how it wasn't really your fault.

SARA: Yeah, it wasn't really. There're, like, kids who do it all the time, but I only shoplifted one skirt, one time, from some big store that never even needed it, and I got in so much trouble. So I signed this thing at court, and they gave me probation, and that's why I went to work at Burger Heaven.

HEIDI: I see, but you said you were going to quit after

the robbery. Why did you stay at Burger Heaven?

SARA: Well, like, before I could quit, Burger Heaven gave me a week off with pay. And they never do that. Then they, like, said I could have a raise if I came back. I guess because they felt bad because I did get shot even if the paramedics said it was only a surface wound. I mean—hey—it was *my* surface! Then with other people quitting, Burger Heaven, they so needed me that I figured I could get the good shifts. Besides, it's like this place already got robbed. It would be some other place's turn next time, right? And I had to work somewhere. So . . . I decided, fine. I might as well stay here instead of some new place that could get robbed next.

HEIDI: So are you working now because you're still on probation?

SARA: No way, like, that whole thing ended four months ago.

HEIDI: Really?

SARA: Oh, yeah, see, there was this letter from the court saying my probation was done. So I start thinking, all right, finally, I'm totally free, and I am so quitting this stupid job.

HEIDI: Yes, but . . .

SARA: But then, Gary, the gorgeous guy who looks just like that guy in Rage, you know, the one who's, like, on the bass guitar. Isn't he just gorgeous? Well, Gary asked me to this party. I mean it was gonna be huge, with lots of older guys, if you know what I mean? Are you, like, married, or do you know what I mean?

HEIDI: I think I understand. So, Gary asked you to this party and . . .

SARA: And I had zero, I mean so *zero*, worth wearing. And for sure, I wasn't shoplifting, because they promised real jail if I, like, did it again. So, I figured what's a few more weeks at Burger Heaven in, like, a whole lifetime, if it means Gary could see me in this black dress that fit so amazing and these four-inch designer heels that practically have my name on them, they're so *me*.

HEIDI: I see, so you kept working to buy the party outfit. But the party was over, and you're still here because . . .

SARA: Well, I do still so want to quit. But it's like if I really want to party, I gotta have the right clothes, and that *so* takes money, and there's just, like, no time to shop and look for a new job and have enough time to meet guys.

HEIDI: So . . . did you stay in touch with the other victims from that night?

SARA: Nope. Most of 'em quit right afterwards, and we weren't really friends anyway. I, like, was always getting written up for not doing stuff like filling up the straws, or not cleaning off the trays, and stuff. Like, now that I think about it, I'm still getting written up.

But you want to, like, know something funny? Last week I opened the mail, and there was this letter to me: "Congratulations! You've been at Burger Heaven long enough to qualify for our management training program." Well, like, at first, I thought, are they kidding me? But then, see, I started thinking that maybe I'll really do it. Because if I'm, like, the manager, I can give the orders to somebody else to clean the gross toilets.

THERESA

Speaker,
Teen Lifeline Training Workshop

Good afternoon, my name is Theresa. I've been a Teen Lifeline volunteer for two and a half years now. I believe that Teen Lifeline is very important, and it can make a big difference to the kids who call.

The training coordinator for new volunteers asked me to speak here because she felt it would be valuable if I shared something I've learned. So, even though I usually don't like to talk about myself, and it's hard for me to do this, I'm going to try.

Last year, at this time, I worked at a Burger Heaven

on Cactus and Tatum. Some of you may remember that there was a hostage situation there. I was one of the hostages. Though I was terrified during the robbery, I went back to school, and I even continued to work at Burger Heaven. I told myself that nothing had changed.

During the day, I was fine, but I began having horrible nightmares. I'd start sobbing so loudly in the middle of the night that my worried mother would rush into my room, holding me as if I were six instead of sixteen.

I had always been the strong one in our family, but when it really came down to it, when I truly had to stand up to fear, I, who thought I was so brave, became just another coward. I willingly surrendered the acting manager that night at Burger Heaven so I could save myself.

Well, anyway, they captured one of the boys who committed the robbery, and I received a letter from the juvenile court saying that the boy had asked for each of us from that night to come to his court hearing so he could apologize to all of us publicly.

I went to the hearing, not because I cared whether that boy apologized to me or not, but because I was so scared of talking to Jordan, the acting manager I had ratted out. I hadn't seen her since that night. I had no idea where she lived. But I figured she would be at the hearing, and I was determined to face my shame and my fear head-on, look her in the eye, and beg for her forgiveness.

Funny thing—Jordan wasn't at the courthouse that day. In fact, none of them went except me and the robber kid—Joe. He looked so small, so scared, that it was hard to believe he had created such terror in all of us.

I've been thinking a lot about fear over this past year and what it can do to people and how foolish it is to feel that a person can never be afraid. Before all this, it was always me who helped my mom, but my meltdown let my mom, for the first time, help me.

It was her suggestion that I leave Burger Heaven. She said we'd survive until I found something that was better for me. And she was right. I found work at a health store and got a job teaching aerobics. I really believe in health and exercise, and having jobs that support my beliefs makes me feel so much better about my work.

Sometimes I'm a little scared of the future, but me and my mom are closer than ever, and I know we'll be okay. In a funny way, I think knowing that no one can be strong all the time has made me a much stronger person.

As I said when I started, I don't usually like to talk about myself, but Teen Lifeline is really important to me. It must be important to you, too, or you wouldn't have given up a Saturday for training. So, I guess the point is that to help others, it's okay at times to let yourself be helped, too.

KEITH

Dear Miss Simcor,

I am glad you didn't forget me. You sent me a birthday card. It is blue. I like blue.

You said this would be my new home. Only it's not new anymore because I have been here for a long time now. I am glad I don't have to live all by myself. My friends, Angie, Stu, Elliott, and—and—I know, and Dominic, and Beth, they live here too. We have houseparents. But they aren't real parents. We don't call them Mom and Dad. We call them by their names. Sandra and Al. They are nice.

Guess what. I'm all grown up! I work. Just like all grown-ups. I clean in a big building. I clean offices on floor fifteen and sixteen and seventeen. Bobby and Jerry help me. I do a very good job. I never forget to empty the wastebaskets. Even when they are hiding under the desks.

I have a secret. I have a girlfriend. She is on TV. She tells me every day when I will need to take my coat to my work or when I won't. I hope I get to meet her, not just on TV. She didn't know it was my birthday. That's why she didn't get me a present. Last year, Jordan didn't get me a present either. I don't like to think about that birthday. It was bad.

This year was good. My houseparents, they got me a present for my birthday. They had a party for me. It was fun. I ate lots of pizza and chocolate cake. Then at work, Bobby and Jerry and the big boss said, "Surprise!" They got me a whole other cake. This one was yellow with white frosting.

I hope you like this letter. It is very long. I worked very hard on it. It took me three nights to write. Sandra helped me. Sandra said I could put the stamp on myself.

I want to tell you something. You are my favorite teacher for always.

Your friend,
Keith

MANUEL AND
MRS. WILKINS

To: Wilkins @bridges.net
From: Manuel@morely.com
Subject: at school

Hey, Mrs. Wilkins,

just a quick e-mail to let you know i'm alive and excited to be here. what a week of firsts!

1. went from never having been outside Arizona to living in Lewiston, Maine

2. went from never even seeing the inside of an airplane to flying across the country. What a trip! (get the pun!)

3. went from never having been in a college dorm to living in one!

my life is so different from anything i could ever have imagined that sometimes i stop and look in mirrors to make sure it is really my reflection looking back at me.—good news—it is!

i'll never be able to thank you enough for everything you did. i know none of this would ever have happened without all your advice and scholarship help. i didn't even know that Bates College existed till u told me!

To: Manuel@morely.com
From: Wilkins@bridges.net
Subject: RE: at school
Hello, Manuel,

It was wonderful to hear from you. I just saw an article that said that Bates was one of the very top liberal arts schools in the whole United States!

I think you'll like living in the dormitory. Do you have a roommate?

I hope you get this e-mail. I'm still not sure how to use the darn computer. Only because you saved my life would I try this whole e-mail kind of communication. I don't like that thing on the computer blinking at me while I'm trying to think. Are you sure you don't want to write regular letters?

To: Wilkins@bridges.net
From: Manuel@morely.com
Subject: More news

hey, mrs. wilkins,

my dorm is called Hedge Hall, and i do have a roommate. he never knew another Latino from Arizona before me, but i guess that's okay because i never knew another white guy from New York—we get along great.

mrs. wilkins, if i can go to college and take classes and live so far away, u can do e-mail.

To: Manuel@morely.com
From: Wilkins@bridges.net
Subject : Re: More News
Manuel,

I am sure it is easier for you to go to college than for me to figure out this e-mail. If my daughter hadn't insisted I move into this senior residence center after the robbery, I wouldn't even live any place that had a computer anywhere in it. I have written this three times now because I am doing something wrong and it erases instead of sends.

To: Wilkins@bridges.net
From: Manuel@morely.com
Subject: I Am The Man!
guess what? guess who just got back his first 2 papers in World Geopolitical Thought and English 101, and guess who got an A on both. WOW!

don't give up on e-mail. u'll get it. isn't that what u always tell me when i'm struggling?

• • •

To: Manuel@morely.com
From: Wilkins@bridges.net
Subject: I'm Learning Too

I think I am finally getting the hang of e-mail. Believe it or not, someone in the residence asked me to help her yesterday, and I actually could do it. Maybe you should become a teacher . . . you taught me so well.

Or maybe you should become a lawyer . . . you kept arguing with me until I finally learned.

Congratulations on your first two papers. I am not surprised. Remember, I taught for 35 years. I know about intelligent students.

To: Wilkins@bridges.net
From: Manuel@morely.com
Subject: who is this guy?

Manuel Alfredo Gonzales sits in small classes of ten students and holds up his end of the discussions.

Manuel Alfredo Gonzales has gone to a ballet, yes, the man has gone to a ballet because of a certain girl he met who wanted to see the ballet. (manuel liked the girl, not thrilled with the ballet)

Manuel Alfredo Gonzales has joined the martial arts club and the water polo club, though he never even heard of water polo before.

Manuel Alfredo Gonzalez—hey—sometimes, i even think of myself in the 3rd person because i am so amazed at all the opportunities that this Manuel Alfredo Gonzales guy has gotten. lol

To: Manuel@morely.com
From: Wilkins@bridges.net
Subject: Questions for You

You haven't said anything about your family. I bet they miss you. Are the leaves starting to turn colors there yet? It's so pretty when that happens. How do you like living in a place that has four seasons? And what's lol?

To: Wilkins@bridges.net
From: Manuel@morely.com
Subject: answers

lol—laughing out loud

leaves haven't turned, but I can't get over all the green here—quite a change from our desert and cactus.

my family doesn't have a computer, but i write to them every week—snail mail. i tell them how amazing college is. i encourage my little sister and brother to study real hard. my mother writes back—every week. Her letters are short and in Spanish. i know what they'll say before i ever open them, but i still love getting them. every week, she says, "Estoy tan orgulloso de ti, mi hijo." my son, i am so proud of you.

To: Manuel@morely.com
From: Wilkins@bridges.net
Subject: Exciting News

Guess what? They have asked me to teach a class to the residents on how to e-mail and use the Internet. Can you believe it? They see me in here on the computers and they think I know so much. That's not true! But I do know more than they do, and it will be fun to teach again.

I can see why your family is so proud of you. I am proud too.

How is working at Burger Heaven? Is the place the same as in Phoenix?

To: Wilkins@bridges.net
From: Manuel@morely.com
Subject: Congrats!

mrs. wilkins . . . back teaching again . . . good for u and lucky for the residents . . . u'll be the same great teacher you always were.

as for burger heaven i'm now a manager in Lewiston 3 nights a week. money helps out a lot—work isn't very hard and i'm still the fastest on drive-through.

bh looks the same as Phoenix, but I don't think about it much . . . except once in a while, especially on a slow night, i hear voices—brings back memories of the robbers—start looking at customers real carefully—feel this nervous grinding in my stomach. i know not even a panic button under the counter, not even the martial arts classes i've mastered could stop everything from ending.

i try to stay so busy that there's no room for those bh memories because this Manuel Alfredo Gonzalez guy—he's counting on a bright future.

DYLAN

Surrounded by idiocy and incompetence, I found myself ultimately ensnared in its web—even after I thought I had successfully escaped. Certainly I deserved to be victorious for overcoming such unreliable partners as dim-witted Greg and pathetic Joe. In fact, though I am not one to praise myself, it was due only to my calm logic that I was able to walk away from the Burger Heaven robbery unscathed and unknown. Others would have panicked and been caught.

Not only did I get away just fine, I was even able to be reasonably punctual for my scheduled purchasing appointment later that night. This was a most important meeting, for from it I planned to acquire the necessary merchandise to open my own business—one better able to provide me with greater and more continued profits than these holdups.

Naturally, I had done my usual due diligence in terms of study and research before selecting this particular dealer's organization. And I must say that, after I decided to work with this group, it took me another two months' time to ingratiate myself enough for them to decide I was worthy of purchasing a significant amount of goods from them.

So how absurd was it that, just as we exchanged the agreed-upon money for merchandise, federal agents swooped down? My well-connected dealer, it seemed, actually had been under police surveillance.

Of course, that was only one of a series of unfortunate ironies. I might have had the funds to pay a worthwhile attorney for my defense instead of an overworked, underinterested court-appointed lawyer, but all my monies had been impounded in the bust. I might have had parents who could have pulled some strings to keep me out of jail, but my parents had no strings to pull. Instead, they only wrung their hands and brought me a Bible. I might have still been only seventeen and thus eligible for a juvenile slap on the wrist, but I had already passed my eighteenth birthday, and besides, I have always looked mature for my age, leaving no "young innocent" for the jury to pity.

Therefore, though I had escaped the robbery with no one being the wiser, I still went to the penitentiary convicted of receiving large amounts of illegal substances.

Rather the most exquisite irony of all, was it not?

Thus, I am currently a guest of the Arizona State Penitentiary. While I cannot claim that these accommodations are particularly pleasant in any way, I have never let my living conditions define me, and I have improved my residence here as much as possible.

Again, it has only been through my own brilliance that this has happened. Upon arriving, I knew I had to immediately establish myself as someone of special importance. I found I was able to convince a few key convicts that I had been a law student, warming up to become a great defense attorney, before I got involved in a drug bust. I had only to drop the most casual of comments about working on getting an "innocent" con a new trial, if I was assured of sufficient protection in jail. I had potential "clients" lining up.

Such a persona worked well in the yard, but it was not appropriate for the warden. By changing my personality mask enough, I was able to convince the guards and the warden that I was basically a good kid who had made one terrible mistake. In tears I manufactured, I confessed to a prison priest that I worried for my soul and hoped to atone for what I had done. I told those in power what they wanted to hear about how much I hoped to study and read and learn and rehabilitate myself in prison.

That is why it was actually no surprise when I found that I had gotten assigned to work in the prison library, where my "job" has left me a goodly amount of time to peruse law books.

In my first few months, the word spread that I had been able to get a guilty counterfeiter a new trial based on a procedural error in the original trial. The truth is that the process for a new trial had already been set in motion before I ever saw the case, but my "client" didn't know that. He thought it was my efforts that were going to get him another chance at freedom. That nicely cemented my reputation as the jailhouse lawyer and ensured not only my own safety, but many little favors that followed.

Now, I sit in the library, left alone by others who mistakenly believe I am about to give them their get-out-of-jail-free card. In all truthfulness, I am working only on one appeal—my own.

However, I am also hedging my efforts by accruing early release time through my exemplary behavior. It is fortunate that there is no conceivable way I can be tied to the six robberies I previously committed. No doubt, early parole would become impossible if multiple crimes were involved. However, as far as anyone will ever know, the receipt of illegal drugs was my only misstep with the law. Though I am a model prisoner, and I have made the best of this unfortunate situation, I do find myself most anxious to end my stay here, and I do not intend to return to confinement.

When I leave this facility, I will carefully craft a life for myself that does not include relying on others. For now I am certain that people—all of them—are all simply too idiotic to be counted on. I have to agree with

Einstein when he said, "Only two things are infinite, the universe and human stupidity, and I'm not sure about the former."

I wish that I could write these thoughts and feelings on paper, for I owe it to the future to document my life. Biographers will want to chronicle my life. However, I also realize that sharing details of my true thoughts is not an option in my current place of residence, so I write this journal only in my mind, and there it will stay until it can be committed to paper as a civilian.

My unique life and the intellect that powers it will, one day, be widely known. Shakespeare said, "Be not afraid of greatness." And I am not, for it is my destiny.

JOE

It is when I close my eyes that I cannot escape the agony of reliving my mother's tear-filled face and my father's horrified gasp. Once again, I am remembering first walking into the courtroom and thinking how small it is and then hoping that maybe it is small because mine was only a little crime.

Sitting in the defendant's chair, it seems as if I am not the one really there. There is a certain sort of numbness as sounds of my trial begin to surround me. A prosecutor speaks, a police officer speaks, and then my attorney. My parents have had to hire him with the money they have been carefully saving for my college education. He has told us that because I am a good kid, without a record, he really doesn't see me being sent to jail, but I'll probably be spending most of my free time in community service.

I am attentive, but there is a sort of fog around me, so that my lawyer has to nudge me when it is finally my turn to speak. I apologize to the court, the police, my parents, and then I turn to apologize to the victims from Burger Heaven. I have asked to do this. Only one of the people from that night has come, and I can't tell from her face what she thinks. Either way, I truly mean every word of how sorry I am.

Then it comes time for the judge's ruling. My attorney and I stand up, and I can feel my knees shaking. The judge states, "Though this young man may have been somewhat of a victim himself, he did commit a crime of his own free will. He did cause bodily harm to another person while in the possession of a handgun."

I can hear the judge's exact tone as he adds, "Despite a recommendation for probation, I feel it is time teens get the message that they are accountable for their actions. While Joe's willingness to apologize to all his victims is commendable, it does not negate his unwise previous choices. He must be made to realize the seriousness of what he did. Fortunately, the young woman he shot was not seriously injured, but she could have just as easily been killed."

And then the ruling: a year in ADJC—juvenile jail.

Maybe I keep replaying this courtroom scene in my brain in the hopes that its outcome will change. I certainly never meant to participate in a real holdup. I hope those people are all okay, and I hope that somehow they have all been able to continue their lives and live their plans.

Unfortunately, the same cannot be said for me. My life has been on hold as I try only to endure another twenty-four hours at a time. On my hand I often write 612. Some guys here are sure that it must have to do with my gang on the outside, but the number is just a statistic I once heard and thought was interesting. Fact: the average person makes six hundred twelve decisions a day. Six hundred and twelve decisions in one day. And on an ordinary day, I made one of those six hundred twelve decisions, which changed the rest of my life.

I don't make many decisions now. Most choices in here are made for us, including such basics as what and when we'll eat and when the lights will come on full blast in the morning or dim at night. Like a robot, I pretty much accept the lack of input I have. What difference does it all make? There is only one decision I really wish could still be mine.

About a month ago, a detective came here to talk to me, said he'd been investigating the string of fast-food robberies from last year, and asked me to break my code of silence and reveal Derrick's whereabouts. I tried to tell him I had no silence code and no idea where Derrick was, but the detective went on as if he hadn't even heard me. He said they had evidence that the masks from those robberies were the same as the ones I'd had when I'd been caught. However, surveillance tapes had shown one of the two individuals from the other robberies was the same size as my partner, but the other was much too tall to be me. Then the cop said, "Joe, you made a really bad decision that got you in this place. Now, be smart and make a better decision that could help get you out early. Help us find Derrick."

I tried to tell that detective that I would if I could, that all I had was the first name Derrick, just like I'd already told the other police officers. But I don't think he believed me. He left saying to let the warden know when I wanted to be smart, and the warden would contact him.

Smart. That word and I don't even belong in the same sentence. Sometimes, I think about what Derrick might be doing now. Probably scamming some other stupid kid somewhere and destroying that kid's life, too. I think maybe I deserved what I got in landing here, but somehow, it seems so unfair that Derrick just got to walk away from everything he did. I don't suppose I'll ever know what happened to him.

I do know that Desert Shadow High and the Joe who attended school there are a part of such different worlds that I'm not sure I could ever return. I ask myself, how could that Joe have been so gullible, so naive? And then I start torturing myself with all these *what ifs*. What if I hadn't gone to English that day? What if I hadn't met Alicia or tried to borrow Jesse's truck or met Derrick or gone along with his plan? And I hate myself all over again.

But today, for the first time since I got here, I have a whole different set of *what ifs*. Like what if there had been one of the all-too-frequent lockdowns today, and what if it had prevented me from going to the juvie jail's version of school? What if the teacher hadn't brought in a bunch of old donated yearbooks from some high school, and instead, had just handed out our usual texts? What if she hadn't told us to look through the yearbook placed on our desk and then write a composition about an activity we saw in it? What if, like most of the others in the class, I'd never even bothered to open the yearbook?

But no one lives in the world of *what ifs*. I guess some small part of me still hopes to get back to the real world with a high school degree. I guess that's why I did as instructed. I paged though the yearbook, feeling miserable from its reminders of the life I didn't have—until my eyes stopped at a page of faces, where one I could never forget stared back at me. And next to that face was a name. Not Derrick . . . but Dylan—Dylan Lynch, his real name. And his face revealed the same self-assured smirk he had worn when we had pulled in to Burger Heaven.

I tore the page out, and for the first time in a very long time, I smiled.

ABOUT THE AUTHOR

TERRI FIELDS says, "I once heard that we make over six hundred decisions every day. Most of those decisions are so routine that we don't even think about them. But what if . . . what if one of those very ordinary decisions resulted in something that would change our entire lives? Wondering about fate and luck and the results of the little decisions we all make became the basis for *Holdup*."

Terri Fields has been a high-school teacher for many years, and got the idea for the setting of *Holdup* from hearing many of her students talk about working in fast-food restaurants. She was named to the All-USA Teacher Team of twenty top teachers in America.

An award-winning author of sixteen books, Terri loves interacting with her readers through author visits in the U.S. and abroad. She and her husband live in Phoenix, Arizona. This is her first book for Roaring Brook Press.

GO FISH

TERRI FIELDS

What did you want to be when you grew up?
As a little girl, I wanted to be an author. However, as I got older, I became too shy to show anyone my writing, so I decided being an author could be a rather unrealistic ambition!

When did you realize you wanted to be a writer?
I remember lining up my stuffed animals on my bed and reading them a book I'd written when I was eight.

What's your most embarrassing childhood memory?
Only one? There are so many! Isn't growing up surviving a series of embarrassments?

What's your favorite childhood memory?
Summer sleep-away camp. I loved every second of it.

As a young person, who did you look up to most?
My mom.

What was your worst subject in school?
Chemistry.

What was your best subject in school?
English and social studies.

What was your first job?
A sales clerk at a department store.

How did you celebrate publishing your first book?
Just seeing it in print was celebration enough!

Where do you write your books?
Mostly, I write at my computer in my office, but I can start a story almost anywhere.

Where do you find inspiration for your writing?
Life. I watch the world around me. There are always lots of ideas for stories.

Which of your characters is most like you?
None of my characters are exactly like me. In *Holdup,* I think Jordan most resembles me, but she's not an exact copy.

When you finish a book, who reads it first?
It depends. I don't have only one person to whom I turn. Often, it is someone in my family.

Are you a morning person or a night owl?
I'm definitely a night owl. I can be ready to write at midnight, but wake me at five or six a.m., and I can barely think.

What's your idea of the best meal ever?
A huge hot fudge sundae from which someone has removed all the calories.

Which do you like better: cats or dogs?
I like both, but I've always had dogs as pets.

What do you value most in your friends?
My friends are such good people who care about others and try to make their lives better. I admire my friends as well as like them!

Where do you go for peace and quiet?
I curl up with a good book, and the world fades away even if it isn't quiet around me.

What's your favorite song?
An old song called "Going Out of My Head."

Who is your favorite fictional character?
Scarlett O'Hara from *Gone with the Wind*, because she never gave up.

What are you most afraid of?
That's a good question. I'm afraid to tell you the answer. ☺

What time of year do you like best?
Winter because I live in Arizona, and our winter is like summer in most places. Our summer is just too hot!

What's your favorite TV show?
I don't have a favorite.

If you were stranded on a desert island, who would you want for company?
My family.

If you could travel in time, where would you go?
I would go to the future to see how life turns out, but I'd only want to do that if everything was going to turn out well.

What's the best advice you have ever received about writing?
Writing is all about rewriting.

What do you want readers to remember about your books?
I want my readers to finish one of my books feeling glad they invested the time and effort to read it.

What would you do if you ever stopped writing?
I hope I never stop!

What do you like best about yourself?
I like the fact that I don't give up easily. I push myself.

What is your worst habit?
I lose things because I don't take enough time to put everything away properly.

What do you consider to be your greatest accomplishment?
I don't know as I accomplished it, but I'm so glad that I have such a close family.

Where in the world do you feel most at home?
Phoenix, Arizona, and Newport Beach, California, but sometimes it's good to travel and not feel so at home.

What do you wish you could do better?
So many things.

Kevin Windor doesn't usually pay attention to the evening news.
But tonight he is. Because Kevin is seeing someone
he knows being carried away in handcuffs.
His father.

Keep reading for an excerpt from
MY FATHER'S SON
available in hardcover from ROARING BOOK PRESS.

breaking news

Ten minutes. Just ten minutes, and then I'll start my pile of waiting homework. I stretch out on the sofa; Mom's not home, so feet up is okay. I press the TV remote, and ominous music with bold words, "BREAKING NEWS," fills the screen. I better pay attention. It could be good for extra credit in Government tomorrow.

I turn up the volume as a woman at a news desk announces, "This just in. In a spectacular development, the alleged DB25 Monster has been arrested. Police apprehended him trying to escape through the bathroom window of 32-year-old Joyce Garlen's apartment. Officers found Ms. Garlen bound and badly beaten, her body bearing the signature DB25 markings. As with other DB25 victims, she had allegedly been tortured and branded before being left to die of her injuries. Ms. Garlen was still alive when police reached her, and she has been rushed to John C. Lincoln Hospital, where she is now in a coma. She is the eleventh known DB25 victim in the tri-state area over the past two years."

Then the camera switches from the anchor to a mug shot of the monster they caught. And it is my face—or least my face as it will look in 30 years. My same thick black hair, my same long eyelashes, my same brown eyes. A new image replaces the full-screen mug shot as I see two cops hustling a hand-cuffed man into the back of a police car.

chapter 1

Two weeks earlier

I AM TRYING TO PAY attention in Spanish. I swear I
am. But it's almost impossible with Emily sitting
only one seat ahead of me. Every day I tell myself,
today's it. Today I'm going to ask her if she wants to
hang out this weekend. But I don't. I guess if I don't
ask, I can keep thinking she'd say yes.

Señora Noyel calls on me. I have no idea what
she's asked. I'm pretty sure though that whether I
answer it in Spanish or English, what I'm daydreaming about Emily is not the answer Señora wants.
"Uh . . . no comprendo," I say.

"Usted no presta la atención," says Señora Noyel.

Not true. I was paying attention . . . to Emily. Señora
Noyel repeats her question and calls on someone
else for an answer. I go back to my thoughts of

Emily until Señora Noyel hands out a paper and tells us to work with our partner to translate it.

The gods were smiling on me the day Señora Noyel assigned Emily as my partner for the semester, definitely the day Spanish became my favorite class. Emily moves her chair real close so we can work on the translation. Right now, it's pretty hard to concentrate because Emily smells so good, but somehow we get the paragraph finished.

Okay, now's the perfect time. I'm going to ask her out. "We're practically the first ones done," I say. "Guess we're a pretty good team." But then my mouth stops short of the date part.

"Yeah, we are a good team." Emily fixes me with her 10,000-megawatt smile and says, "Great that it's Friday, huh?"

"Sure is . . . don't know how we'd survive without weekends."

"So," she looks at me with her big blue eyes. "Are you going to hang out at Cliff's tomorrow night?"

Jason mentioned that people were going to Cliff's, but I thought it was just some guys to play a little b-ball. Suddenly, the weekend seems a whole lot more interesting. "Uh . . . you going?" I ask.

"Well . . . I thought I might if certain other people planned to go . . ." She stops speaking, but her eyes hold mine.

"Yeah, well, I might be there." I'm trying to be cool about this, but maybe that was too cool. I want to be there with her. "Yeah. Actually, I guess I'm going for sure." My voice almost squeaks. This girl turns me into pathetic.

But Emily doesn't laugh at me or roll her eyes. She just says, "Great! If you're there, it'll be lots more fun."

I grin. Life is good. After school, when Jason and I meet up, I punch his arm. "Hey," he says, "trying to disable your teammate?"

"Hey yourself," I reply. "How come you failed to mention girls going to Cliff's?"

Jason shrugs. "Guess I was waiting for you to tell me you had to stay home and study Pre-Cal, and then I was going to spring it on you to see if it changed your mind."

"Very funny." I say. "It's not like I study all the time. It's just that you never study at all."

"And I'm a better man for it," Jason proclaims.

"Yeah, but *your* dad hasn't already made plans to go to the Harvard-Yale game when he visits you at Yale."

Jason yawns. "Scottsdale Community College is fine by me. So how'd you hear about the girls?"

I shrug. I try to make it sound unimportant. "Emily mentioned it."

"Whoa!" Jason sighs. "You know, if I weren't

your best friend, and you didn't have it so bad for her, I'd . . ."

I interrupt. "I don't have anything so bad for anyone."

"Great," he says. "Then you won't care if I hit on her?"

"Stay away from Emily."

Jason laughs. "Uh, huh. That's what I thought. You got it bad, my man. Well, at least you recognize a truly hot girl. Want to head over to Cliff's together?"

I shake my head. "I'm staying at my dad's this weekend. I'll probably just drive myself over."

By Saturday night, what I am driving myself is crazy. It's hard to know what girls think looks good. I stand staring at the closet. Finally, I pull on my green shirt. I go to grab the shoes I want from the closet, and I realize they're at Mom's. These loafers will have to do. Living in two places means the stuff I need is always at the other house. My clothes are minimal at Dad's since I'm only here some weekends.

I reach for my aftershave and realize that it's empty. "Great!"

Dad hears me. "Can I help with something?"

I hold up the empty bottle.

"Ahh . . . so tonight isn't about basketball with the guys, huh? You know . . . I used to use that aftershave, but I found something I think is better. Try this . . ." He brings in a dark blue bottle. "Want to tell me about her?"

I shrug. "Just a girl at school. Nothing special."

Dad grins. He knows me too well. "Yeah, well, nothing special is one lucky lady if you're interested. Have fun tonight."

I sigh. "I hope so."

Dad laughs. "I'd give you the whole every-guy-has-trouble-figuring-out-girls-in-high-school speech, but I think I've already done that. And as I remember, the last time I shared my great wisdom on women, you were less than impressed."

I smile. I don't remember any such conversation, but maybe I wasn't listening. I check my cell phone for the time. I don't know if it'd be better to get to Cliff's before Emily so she has to come up to me or after she's already there so it doesn't seem like I'm hanging out looking for her.

"I won't wait up for you," Dad calls as I grab my keys and head for the door. "Good luck!"

Dad's so great that way. I never have to answer a thousand questions. If this had been Mom, she'd have wanted to know if Cliff's parents would be home; she'd have asked who else was going. She'd have kept prodding me for the name of the girl I liked. Dad just keeps life simple.

* * *

Cliff lives in an old beige stucco house set back from the street. It has a huge backyard and a great blacktop area for basketball. There've been a few other times when girls have been here . . . so I don't know what the big deal is for me about tonight. Except as I think about it, the last time girls were over, I hung out playing basketball and pretty much ignored them. Of course, that was before Emily.

By the time I get to Cliff's tonight, I've got the whole sweaty palms thing. I walk into the backyard, trying to look around without being obvious. I don't see Emily, but there are a lot of people, and it's kind of dark, so it's hard not to stare and still see anything. Suddenly, I feel a sharp poke in my ribs. "Be still his beating heart, his true love isn't here."

"Knock it off, Jason!" I poke him back.

He laughs. "So . . . I guess no basketball tonight."

"Is that because you don't want to get beat?" I bluff.

"Are you kidding? Me worry about getting beat by you?"

"Not kidding, not a worry, just a fact," I say.

"Is that so?" He glances at my feet. "Nice shoes for b-ball," Jason smirks. "Looks like you got dressed for other games tonight."

I know my face is getting red, and so I shoot back, "Uh, well . . . you move so slow, I don't need basket-ball shoes. Truth is . . . I could be wearing flip-flops and beat you."

"Flip-flop . . . flip-flop. Is that the beating of the boy's heart when he hears about Emily?"

"Nope. Flip-flop, flip-flop; that's you on the ground after I've made a killer crossover."

I try to glance around without Jason's noticing. I don't see Emily. I could go look for her, but . . .

"I think your girlfriend may have stood you up," Jason says.

"Hey! I keep telling you, she's not my girlfriend."

"That's because she's got good taste in guys."

"Oh, like you'd know anything about that!"

Then I hear, "Want some popcorn?" I turn around to see Emily holding out a bowl to share.

"Thanks," Jason says, reaching for a handful. I'm going to kill him. Really, I am. He pays no attention to my signals and keeps talking to Emily. It takes about ten minutes before he finally gets the hint that three's a crowd and disappears. The moon is out; the night is nice, and when a slow song starts, I get up my courage and ask Emily if she wants to dance. We join the other swaying couples up on the patio, and as I put my arms around Emily and her face leans into my shoulder, I think that life doesn't get much better. While there's part of me wishing we could be like a few of the couples really going at it on blankets over by the bushes, on the whole, it's pretty great just to talk and laugh and hold Emily's hand.

Emily seems like she's having a good time. We talk about school and TV and movies and stuff. As the party starts to break up, I blurt out, "So, I could take you home if you want. I mean . . . first we could get something to eat or something." It isn't too smooth, but at least it's out there.

Emily smiles at me. She really does have the greatest smile of any girl anywhere. "Kev . . . that sounds great, but I'm spending the night at Callie's. I've got to go home with her. I promised. It was a great idea though. I'm really sorry."

If she's sorry, I'm even sorrier. We're both sitting on this lawn chair sort of off from the crowd. I have my arm around Emily, and she's snuggled in next to me. Her cologne or something smells so good. She looks up at me, "Tonight's been nice, huh?"

I take that as my cue to lean over and kiss her. And the kiss is every bit as good as I imagined it would be.

I don't want to, but I walk Emily out to Callie's car and watch her leave. But then I start letting myself think about tonight, think about how maybe Emily might want to be more than just my Spanish partner, which me gusta muy mucho!